THE BEECH FOREST

MARLIS WESSELER

The Beech Forest

Thistledown
Press

Thistledown Press Ltd.
Unit 222, 220 20th Street W
Saskatoon, SK
S7M 0W9
www.thistledownpress.com

Library and Archives Canada Cataloguing in Publication

Title: The beech forest / by Marlis Wesseler.
Names: Wesseler, Marlis, 1952– author.
Identifiers: Canadiana 20230559662 | ISBN 9781771872546 (softcover)
Subjects: LCGFT: Novels.
Classification: LCC PS8595.E63 B44 2024 | DDC C813/.54—dc23

Cover photograph: ©iStockPhoto/Kenneth Schulze
Cover and book design by Ingrid Paulson
Printed and bound in Canada

Thistledown Press gratefully acknowledges the financial assistance of
The Canada Council for the Arts, SK Arts, and the Government of
Canada for its publishing program.

Canada Council   Conseil des arts
for the Arts   du Canada

Canadä   Saskatchewan

For Evan

ONE

On one of the last autumn nights of the visit, Lisa Braun dreams she is Jewish. When she wakes up, she can hear Gerhardt talking, the murmur of Karl's answer, Renata's clear laughter. Despite the dream, she finds the sound of German being spoken indistinctly from another room comforting. It reminds her of visits with her mother's sisters, especially Aunt Gemma who, as the eldest of a large family, retained a German...not accent exactly. What would you call it? Certainly not a lilt. A sound from the back of the throat that could be distinguished even when they all spoke English.

The apartment is old enough to still feature a toilet with a little raised ceramic shelf. This morning it bothers her, just the sight of it. German self-obsession. She gazes into the mirror over the sink that's a bit too high for her, brushing out her brown hair cut in a bob that is now growing too long. Maybe she should get it cut here. She notices some new strands of grey, examines the crow's feet behind her glasses. Her nose is becoming hawklike, just like her dad's.

She practises a bright German *Guten Morgen* before heading to the living/dining room, hoping for a newly made pot of coffee. The apartment is furnished in blond wood with leather couches and chairs, and glass vases from Sweden are placed attractively around the room. Paintings of scenic views grace cream-coloured walls. Everything shines with the beauty of regular and impeccable housekeeping.

"*Morgen!*" Her mother-in-law looks up from buttering a roll. Renata is now, in her seventies, beginning to put on weight, but she dyes her hair the blonde it has been all her life, and likely anyone who knew her in her twenties would still recognize her.

Karl, white haired and thin, glances at Lisa with his usual benign irony and asks if she has slept well.

"*Ja, sehr gut.*" She smiles and nods, takes her place at the table, and lets them get on with their conversation, exchanging looks with Gerhardt, whose "good morning" shows an undertone of irritation. After three weeks, he is beginning to find the constant conversation an effort and clearly feels she's not doing her part. "Have you checked your email yet?" she asks during a rare lull, wondering if there's been any word from their son, who is also in Europe, travelling with his girlfriend. They are supposed to show up for a visit before she and Gerhardt go home.

"Yes," he says. "Nothing from Tyler."

Disappointed, she takes a roll from the basket, cuts it in half, and tries to decide which of the variety of spreads and cut meats and cheeses she wants. She will pass as usual on the *Hackfleisch* which, no matter what you call it, is nothing but raw hamburger. "I think I'll go for a walk in the woods this morning," she announces in German, avoiding her husband's eyes. She butters her roll carefully. "I need some exercise." She adds quickly in English to Gerhardt, "On my own."

"Good," he says crisply. "That's fine." He pours himself more coffee and turns his attention to his mother's story about an eccentric neighbour.

••

THE APARTMENT BUILDING is on the outskirts of a small town about an hour from Berlin, in the former Eastern bloc and on the edge of a beech forest. People in the neighbourhood walk in the forest for exercise, to find peace and quiet, to commune with nature. Nature seems to be very important to Germans, maybe because they haven't conserved much of it.

Today the weather is fine, but since it's a weekday the woods are almost deserted. She stops to sit on a fallen log, admiring the trees, which seem to thrive in Germany mainly among their own kind, unlike the scrub brush at home where pine and poplar, spruce and the odd willow compete for the same sparse nutrients.

This forest is extraordinarily beautiful, and she wishes she had a sketchbook with her, sorry for the first time in years that she gave up painting. Silver-grey beech trees with velvet bark rise, monumental, from the brown earth. Perfect sprays of oval leaves filter the light from above like stained glass, casting emerald clarity on the forest floor. But in spite of the September light, the ground here harbours little but an assortment of last year's leaves, the odd decaying log like the one on which she is resting, and a few branches. Few ferns or bushes grow here, no excess of any kind. Nothing but beech trees. And even with her bad sense of direction, it isn't easy to get lost here. Everything, nature itself, seems well-planned and precise.

The German word for 'beech forest'? *Buchenwald*. No wonder she dreamed about being Jewish, especially after all the TV documentaries last year marking the sixtieth anniversary of the end of the war. She can't recall anything much from the dream except that newly discovered heritage and a certain bewilderment.

Her in-laws haven't lived in their apartment very long, but when they refer to *der Buchenwald*, there's no hitch to their voices,

no self-conscious undertone. To them it's just a word for the neighbouring woods. It is next door to them, they go for walks in it, it is
as ordinary as *der Kieferwald*, the pine forest down the road where
they hunt for mushrooms, and which is supposedly off-limits to the
public because of undetonated ammunition left over from the
Russians.

A voice calling from the other side of a small brook startles her. It
rings alarmingly cheerful, almost exactly like that of her mother-in-
law. Even though she knows Renata to be entertaining her son at
home, she stands up and walks the other way, leaving the main path.

Now that his parents are older, she and Gerhardt should take
more trips to Germany. But visiting Karl and Renata is always
exhausting because Renata insists on just that: visiting. Lisa has to
leave the apartment or stay in bed if she wants any time to relax.
She's rarely left to read for more than half an hour at a time, or to
relax in front of the TV. Even during past visits when they had the
kids with them, Tyler and Stephanie could laze around, listlessly
reading comic books, but she and Gerhardt had to chat.

Having constantly to concentrate on a second language tires
her out, but it isn't only all the loquaciousness that bothers her.
Karl and Renata talk about their other in-laws with such gleeful
spite that she is sure they often mock her too. And in restaurants,
visits to the city, on short holidays by the sea, they laugh at strangers, right out in the open. Shy Swedes passing awkwardly by
their table, swaddled Turks crossing the street in front of them,
fat people on the beach, people who walk funny. Conspicuous
chortles or simple har-harring that she hates having anything to
do with. She's noticed this in other Germans too. Not all, of course,
but enough. Not anything like a Canadian's way of raising a quick
eyebrow, widening eyes so slightly that only their friends, supposedly, would notice. It isn't that her countrymen are any kinder,

but their derision is subtler. It could take years before a foreigner grew to hate Canadians.

She recalls taking Tyler to skating lessons in Saskatoon years ago, and a couple of men next to her tying their kids' skates, one saying to the other, "Cold enough for you?" and the other replying, "But it's a dry cold." No grins, no sly glances at each other. Only another Canadian would know they were mocking the banal small talk of a couple of grandparents nearby. She's retained this exchange from years ago because even at the time it typified something to her.

Gerhardt also appreciates quiet Canadian sarcasm in spite of the fact that it could well be directed at him. Berliners are famous, at least in Germany, for their dry humour, although they tend to laugh at their own jokes. With only a few exceptions, usually late at night over too much alcohol, the Brauns' stories of the war and its aftermath are all told with a certain black amusement.

Almost every one of them is about hunger: The pig they kept hidden in the house, fattening him as well as they could until he got big enough to butcher. They named him Putzi, he was so clean, Renata said, and he would make little snoring noises when they scratched behind his ears. They almost couldn't bring themselves to slaughter him.

Or later on, when the East German *Stasi* in their new uniforms came to search their place for stolen vegetables. "Turnips!" Renata said to them. "You're spending, wasting time here looking for turnips?" They could tell she wasn't lying, looked around and left. Afterwards, she became hysterical when Karl showed her the cache of turnips hidden beneath a floorboard under the couch.

The time they'd been invited over to the neighbours' for stew, only to realize that their hosts weren't eating much, and the family's little dog was missing.

Early on they showed her an old photo album that included pictures of an uncle of Renata's sporting a Nazi uniform. When Lisa came to those pages there was an almost imperceptible watchfulness, a slight stiffening of spines. She was too young then to think much of it. She thought every family in Germany must have some Nazi relative or other, and now she knows it's true. People joined the Nazi party because it was expected: businessmen who didn't want to fail, teachers who wanted to keep their jobs. On the other hand, not everyone would have worn a uniform. She'd meant long ago to ask Renata more about the uncle, but the subject never seemed to come up.

She finds herself in a weedier-looking section of forest where the beech trunks are narrow, younger, and less beautiful than the ones she's just left. Maybe she has succeeded in getting lost. Like Dante, hah, only she is well past the middle of her life, unless she lives to be over a hundred. Or Hansel and Gretel. After stumbling more than once on exposed roots, she finds another path that looks well used, almost as if it has been swept. Hansel and Gretel would be out of luck looking here for signs of their previous whereabouts, but then again their forest had been entirely different. They were lost in the mossy dark woods of Germany's beginnings, apocryphal children caught vandalizing someone's shelter. In spite of the cool autumn shade, she steams with sudden heat and takes off her jacket. Maybe the fairy tale was based on a menopausal sorceress, someone who decided the deep woods would be a good place to find refuge, set up her oven, and live the rest of her days in peace, working on her own gingerbread creations.

Stoves and ovens seem to crop up often in German fairy tales: the source of domestic comfort and nourishment; a means of rendering; a way to burn evidence. Lisa's own heritage is half German.

Her mother's parents immigrated to Canada in the early twentieth century. So did her father's parents, but from Denmark. Gerhardt was welcomed so warmly into her family he was astonished.

Gehr-Heart. After so many cycles of love, anger, contentment, hate, passion, boredom, contempt, affection, comfort, all now diluted by years, by tiredness, by the familiarity within all long marriages, she still loves the sound of her husband's name.

She walks aimlessly now, dragging her feet, knowing she should get back before lunch, regretting that she hasn't lost her way. She wants an excuse to be late. She hears signs of civilization, people talking in a clearing straight ahead, and veers off onto a less well-travelled path. She follows it only to find herself at a faux-medieval restaurant where she can get beer and a sandwich. She might as well give up trying to get lost. And of course, she can always let Gerhardt know where she is anyway—the new cell phone is in her bag.

"I'm at a little café in the *Buchenwald.* I'm going to have lunch here."

"By yourself?"

"No. Me and my entourage." Whenever they travel, he treats her as mentally deficient because she's absent-minded and has no sense of direction. At least now that his parents are getting old he is more preoccupied with them, running errands for Renata, who recently had a health scare with her heart. Lisa feels extraneous, as usual. But of course that's nobody's fault but her own.

Sitting at a little picnic table in the sunlight, she admires the restaurant's perfect squareness and fake medieval beams, its art-fully casual stucco. She takes a long drink of Pilsner from a delicate, gold-rimmed glass and examines the menu. Maybe tomorrow she'll continue to insist on some time to herself and go into Berlin, tour the art galleries. There's a Max Ernst retrospective she really wants to see, and then, since she'll be at the modern gallery anyway, she'll tour the *Gemäldegalerie* with its Old Masters. The two buildings are situated so close together you can buy one ticket for both, and she will do that, even though she knows trying to pack too much art into a few hours never pays off.

She saw a play once in Calgary—what was the name of it? The main character said you can only comprehend (or was it apprehend?) one artifact or work of art in a day, take one image away with you to keep as your own. And it's true, if she thinks of all the art galleries and museums she has visited in her travels, each one might as well have contained one object: the exquisite Botticelli with ugly feet on that first visit to the *Gemäldegalerie*; the intricate Chinese vase in the Victoria and Albert when she was working in London; the Bosch in the old Dahlem before the Wall came down; the Rosetta Stone in the British Museum; the poppies in the Van Gogh. Still, she's disappointed in herself for recalling only the Mona Lisa in the Louvre, with its glass cover reflecting tourists' flashbulbs.

In the Museum of Modern Art in New York, she'd come across a small Max Ernst sculpture set modestly on the floor that she found so uplifting she wanted to take it home. Called *Lunar Asparagus*, it was a white stalk topped by an eyeless face with an excruciatingly silly grin. You could see that it was basking in moonlight. Or was it growing on the moon and basking in earthlight? Whatever had inspired Ernst to create such a thing, it was one of the few art objects she'd ever coveted to the point of real desire. She knew the idea was absurd, but she thought if somehow she were able to obtain that sculpture, to be greeted with that grin every single morning, she could be happy. She would keep it, ill-gotten or not, and set it up in her living room beside the houseplants.

Hungry after her walk, she decides to order *Sauerbraten* with potato pancakes. She gives a little wave to the waitress, who is wearing the ubiquitous milkmaid outfit. Nobody here ever seems to wonder why food servers dress like someone who works in a barn.

Yes, she will take the train to Berlin tomorrow and hope to find her asparagus again. Spending a whole day by herself will cheer her up.

TWO

She picks up a pamphlet in the gallery foyer and is delighted to read *Lunar Asparagus, 1935* on the list of exhibits. She smiles broadly at the museum worker guarding the entrance, who after a tired double-take, slightly modifies his scowl. She wanders through the various decades of Ernst's work, past dream landscapes of sinister forests, desert hoodoos, lush Dali-like interiors, past the beach scenes featuring silver-grey buttocks she thinks of as his Buns of Steel paintings, and finds the painted bronze figure, rather dimly lit, set up on a stand in a corner of the room. The name plate says *Lunar Asparagus*, but it isn't the one from the MoMA. From the base of this statue grow two stalks, not just the one. Both heads have surreal, spacey expressions. Worse, the face she clearly recalls and thought she wanted has lost its joyous goofiness. It has something of a mouth, and the mouth is sort of grinning, but it isn't the same.

How could her memory be so faulty? Well, it can't be, she decides. Her lone asparagus must still be there, sitting by itself in the MoMA, waiting for her to visit New York City again. It must be part of a series of lunar asparagus.

She drifts distractedly through the remainder of the Ernst exhibit and outside into a grey fall day, onto a giant grey cement patio, past stone and steel and cement statues, down to the side-walk and walks a block or so to the stone-and-cement-sided *Gemäldegalerie.*

Inside, she feels disoriented, overwhelmed by the vast central hall's blond hardwood parquet, its golden pathways leading to rooms of priceless treasures. She walks through the labyrinth of nationalities and centuries, almost entirely alone with the Old Masters except for the museum guards who, taking their jobs seri-ously, keep a wary eye on her from one room to the next. A jaded lethargy begins to slow her down long before she finds the Italian Renaissance she is looking for.

The image she will take away with her this time is from one of the sixteenth-century Flemish still-lifes of overripe fruit beside dead pheasants or hares. The sparkle of crystal glasses, the dark shine of cherries, the finely delineated fuzz on the peaches, the green glow of grapes, the flaccid, absolute deadness of the game. How can the vibrancy of these colours, the quality of this painted light have lasted through all these centuries?

Outside again in the late afternoon, continuing to stroll aim-lessly, she grabs a snack at a *Currywurst* stand and realizes she isn't sure anymore where she can catch a bus back to the train station. The map Renata had offered her was too big to fit in her purse, so she said she would find one at the station. She didn't. She simply followed some German tourists, who she knew from their conver-sation were on their way to the same galleries she was, off the train and onto the right bus.

She can't ask the snack vendor for directions. He is now ignor-ing her completely and mumbling under his breath because he doesn't understand her accent. She glances at his sullen face, his misshapen woolen sweater, and is happy enough just to walk away with her hot dog without being yelled at.

She knows Gerhardt has little confidence she will manage to make it here and back on her own and will be standing by with his cell phone, ready to borrow his father's car to come and pick her up, or to arrange for his sister to do so from work. When he put her on the train heading toward the city, he said gloomily, half-teasing, that he could only hope for the best. "Unlike you," she told him, "I'm not allergic to asking directions." Right now, however, the Berliners tramping past in their anoraks and walking shoes or stodgy business attire do not look inviting enough to accost with questions.

The bus stop is around here somewhere. She could take a cab to the train station if worse comes to worst. She doesn't want to risk trying the subway; she can picture herself missing the terminal where she's supposed to transfer, condemning herself to hours of subterranean purgatory.

A half hour later, there are no cabs in sight, and she is totally lost. Why, when she wanted to get lost yesterday in the woods and couldn't, would she lose her sense of direction so entirely in the city? She is sadly familiar with this situation, but it always weighs heavily, providing a distant sense of self-disdain, as if part of her were some relative giving a lecture. As if part of her were Gerhardt. She knows she's turned several wrong ways, and now finds herself in a small cobblestone plaza frequented mainly by people walking right through, people who undoubtedly know where they are going. Surrounded by empty benches, a young man painted all in silver is pretending to be a statue for a couple of teenagers and three pigeons, all eyeing him speculatively.

She decides against asking anything of the unisex teenagers, who in spite of sporty-looking running shoes and jackets wear green Mohawks. Neither fish nor fowl, as her Aunt Gemma would say. She stands there pretending to examine her cell phone until they saunter off. The pigeons lose interest too, migrating to a garden plot off to the side, and she is left alone to study the statue for signs of life. She looks in her purse for euros—what would be appropriate?

"Can you tell me how to get to the bus stop for the *Ostbahnhof?*" she asks in German. He doesn't move. She rustles a five-euro note half out of her wallet.

"For ten euros I will help walking you there," he says in English.

"Oh, you don't need to do that," she says without conviction. "Just give me good directions."

"Ach, I am finishing for today. This is not the season, no one is stopping. It was a stupid idea." Ten euros is too much, but she gives him the money. He gathers up the few coins he'd managed to collect and leads her out of the plaza, going the opposite way she would have turned if she'd been by herself.

"I have no sense of direction whatsoever," she says, glumly attempting conversation. A handsome man in a perfectly tailored grey suit passes by, giving them a wide berth.

"Many women don't," he says. She feels she should defend her sex somehow from her own failings, but doesn't comment. She remembers Gerhardt and their neighbour Robbie laughing when the province was forced to hire a certain percentage of women to fight forest fires. The men complained they would spend more time looking for lost women than fighting fires.

"That paint must get uncomfortable," she says. "And standing all day without moving. I don't know how you do it."

"I only did come for two hours or so here," he says. "The season is past, but I needed money." His plastic armour squeaks as he moves, while his bare arms, legs, and face, covered in greasepaint and a kind of sparkly powder, shed tiny glints. His chin is cleft with a Kirk Douglas dimple.

"Are you an actor?" she asks.

"Yes!" He glances at her with a flicker of energy. "I am searching always for new roles."

She wonders if this means he is actively involved in a theatre, or if he is always unemployed and looking for work. Or if he simply looks on life as a stage. If he takes the bus or subway home, shedding flecks all the way. If he has a wife or a roommate who paints him, or if there is a street performers' guild of some kind where he goes to become gilded—ha—where he has a locker for his clothes and somebody to hose him off. But her powers of conversation flag, along with her curiosity. People look at them with amusement or irritation or with nothing, a nanosecond of a bored flicker.

He points out a bus stop across a wide boulevard. This isn't the one she remembers, but he tells her what number to take. They shake hands goodbye, and when she is finally seated on the bus, having first double-checked with the driver, she notices silver embedded in the lifeline of her palm.

The train is crowded at the end of the day, and she has to sit the wrong way, facing a man reading a newspaper with the giant headlines of the *Berliner Morgenpost*. She wishes she had something to read. She can't get over a slight queasiness when she looks out the window only to see scenery she's already passed. The outskirts of the city meld with farmers' fields that are almost as flat and featureless as those in Saskatchewan. She closes her eyes and thinks of the art galleries, of the still-life paintings showing the brevity of existence, and about her asparagus that wasn't there.

When her in-laws all lived in the city, she was disappointed at the small amount of time she and Gerhardt were allowed to spend in galleries and jazz clubs. Except for their trip to Berlin soon after their marriage, most holidays were taken up with nothing but visiting, and even during that first trip most of their outings involved sightseeing. The Wall was still there then, of course. It was one of the tourist attractions you couldn't avoid. Normal-seeming streets, pavement over cobblestone, would suddenly lead to a dead end: dirty grey cement topped with barbed wire, worms of sprayed graffiti providing the only colour. Every few hundred yards, wooden-faced soldiers were stationed, at attention, watching from tall stands that resembled lifeguard towers. Death guards.

In later years, as soon as the Wall came down, vast and obsessive construction and restoration began. It is still going on, will continue for decades; centuries for all she knows. West German ants took over, her in-laws said, and East German grasshoppers struggled. Used to the lackadaisical rhythms of a communist work ethic, unemployable and bewildered, the *Ost Deutschlanders*, the "Ossies," would take at least a generation to catch up.

In the seventies and eighties, the divided city contained an atmosphere of pragmatic sophistication that she appreciated. The contours of the Wall were always there even when it was out of sight, an antidote to optimism. She recalls how glamorous and European she felt sampling Berliner beer in restored pubs, grooving to Pat Metheny in Quasimodo, walking along cobblestone side streets imagining herself following in the footsteps of Marlene Dietrich or Greta Garbo. Wishing she could have seen Berlin the way it had been before the war, before everything old was bombed. She wanted to frequent decadent cabarets, to dance on the black-and-white tile of the Grand Hotel.

Every couple of days on that first trip, Karl or Peter, Gerhardt's brother-in-law, drove them to a different section of town, Gerhardt in the passenger side while she sat in the back with his grandmother. The family considered sightseeing a chance to kill two birds with one stone: entertain Lisa, and take Oma for outings. Whenever they passed the Wall, it was pointed out: "*Da. Da ist die*

Mauer." It was said with a certain pride, she thought, intermingled with a satisfied sense of communal self-pity. Berliners had long ceased to feel horror or sorrow whenever they passed it, simply because it had been there so long it had become ordinary. It was an inconvenience that couldn't be helped, rather like bad weather. In fact, she realized, Berliners pointed out the Wall in much the same way people from Saskatchewan spoke about winter.

"Sometimes it's forty below," she found herself saying to Peter.

"*Mein Gott, das ist wie in Siberien!*" he exclaimed, and she nodded smugly, pleased.

The only one who didn't seem used to the Wall was the grandmother, who would resolutely look at something else, or down at her lap.

The first time Lisa had met Gerhardt's family all gathered together, she'd been overwhelmed by hearty handshakes and laughter and enthusiastic guttural speech accompanied by touches to kneecaps, wrists, shoulders. They were exhausting and bewildering. The grandmother sat ignoring everyone, gazing silently at her own thoughts, and Lisa joined her on the couch and made hesitant conversation in her rudimentary German. Two quiet foreigners in exuberant territory. Oma had the smoothest skin she had ever seen on someone so old. Not that she looked young, it was just that her face hadn't wrinkled. It was round and smooth, with slightly sagging cheeks and a few broken veins creating faint blotches.

The old woman warmed to her and reminisced about her girlhood, conjuring up stories of dances and fairy-tale evenings of frosted drinks at summer spas, *Glühwein* around the fireplace at winter resorts in the Alps. When she was a girl, she said, her hair was so long she could sit on it. Her *Papa* absolutely refused to let her have it cut. She used to play the piano at friends' houses, her back straight, as she had been taught, white hands held delicately above the keys, wrists flexible and dainty, her long chocolate-brown hair almost touching the carpet. She remembered herself in a white dress with a red sash, a red ribbon in her hair, her father so fondly proud. "Ach, but now I am an old woman," she said, patting Lisa's hand and smiling.

Toward the end of that first trip, Lisa and Gerhardt visited his grandmother at her home. She rented an apartment in a modern building where other elderly people lived, and managed to keep her beige carpet, the flowered couch, the china cabinet, and all the other furniture and knick-knacks spotless, with little outside help.

She greeted them at the door with energy and enthusiasm and fed them *Rouladen* for supper. After dessert, she sat down comfortably with her brandy and started reminiscing. Gerhardt's parents rarely discussed the war seriously, although his mother had once said, about the concentration camps with their high walls and barbed wire, "We didn't know what went on; we had no idea," and Lisa believed her. But late in the evening, his grandmother spoke in slow, direct German, looking straight at Lisa. "When I was a girl we were a rich family. Then came the Depression and the inflation, and we were ruined by Jewish speculators. Others as well as us. By Jews. Jews were not popular—we called them pigs. Then Hitler came and they all disappeared."

Lisa watched Gerhardt's expression change from that of shock to apology (she's only an old lady) to belligerence (she's here and she's my grandmother, whether it suits you or not). He stood up and thanked her for supper and said they had to get back.

She nodded, looking closely again at Lisa's face before she kissed her goodbye. "Most of us say we didn't know what was happening back then," the old woman said, "but we knew enough. We knew what to turn our backs to."

On the way to his parents' apartment, Gerhardt said, "She's had a hard life. Her parents lost everything and died in poverty when she was young, and the Russians killed her husband in a work camp after the war. My grandfather. Then she lost her house in East Germany. She calls the Russians *Schwein* too."

"And that's supposed to make everything fine? That she calls the Russians pigs *too*?"

They drove on in silence, then Lisa asked, "Did I understand everything? Did—"

"Remember, she's eighty years old," he interrupted. "Who knows what goes on in her mind?" His voice was harsh and resentful—against her, she realized, not his grandmother. "Anyway, I didn't hear all she said."

Leaning her head back on the headrest, she closed her eyes and thought, Fine, this will be the end of it. A newscaster on the car radio was speaking German too quickly for her to follow. She wanted to be able to tune the radio to Peter Gzowski's mellow but earnestly Canadian voice. Thinking of that voice made her want to cry.

At the time, she thought it was only a holiday. That in a few days they'd leave it all behind.

Years later, watching a documentary on the war, Gerhardt said Hitler could never have succeeded in Canada. "Canadians are too sarcastic. They would mock him out of the running long before he gained any real power."

She isn't sure what he thinks now. Gerhardt rarely stuck to one opinion for very long, which was one of the many surprises in his character she'd had to grow used to. She doesn't know if, given the same circumstances, Canadians would support someone like Hitler. But she knows hearth and home are sacrosanct to Germans, even more than Americans' motherhood and apple pie. She has the impression that the outside world is important to Germans only as necessary background to themselves and their families, held in scornful and, since the war, defensive suspicion until proven benign.

At the end of that first trip, when she and Gerhardt were ready to return to Canada, his mother told him to clean out his closet, to take what he wanted and she'd get rid of the rest. On the flight home, he wore a beautiful iron-grey leather trench coat he'd bought at a flea market when he was a teenager. It fit as if it had been made for him. She said it looked like something Humphrey Bogart would have worn. No, he said, it was from the war. It had belonged to an SS officer. For a while in the sixties, it was the in thing for hippie types to buy these old overcoats and wear them as some sort of statement. He grimaced with disdain at his old self, but still, he wore the coat. She tried to imagine it exuding an aura of corruption, of terror, but couldn't. It was just a coat, worn by her new husband, who looked spectacular in it. But when they got home, he never put it on, not once. Eventually, it did begin to give her the creeps, hanging there in the back of the closet as if it belonged. She said she didn't want it there anymore and told Gerhardt to get rid of it, she didn't care how. It disappeared. She is still sometimes uncomfortable with the idea that some nut obsessed with Nazi paraphernalia might have found it in a Salvation Army store.

Used to riding backward on the train now, she watches the flat Brandenburg landscape and darkening sky with a dull ache in her throat, not of nostalgia but of regret she can't identify. She feels somehow that her life is over. Well, not her life, but her capacity for joy.

It's likely just fluctuating hormones. And it doesn't help to know that Tyler is somewhere in Europe but not bothering to make the detour to Germany. She's sure this is his girlfriend Céline's fault. And then of course there is Stephanie. The anxiety about her daughter is always there, whether she's conscious of it or not.

Enough. She could at least use time spent on another continent as a vacation away from Stephanie, away from fretting over the same old regrets.

The man across from her puts down his newspaper and she closes her eyes again. She still has to deal with being a guest of her in-laws for another few days. She longs to be in her own house or outside in the garden cleaning up fall debris, enjoying the asters and chrysanthemums. At home now, she and Gerhardt live more or less amiably and very quietly. She has little social life. It's too much of an effort to drive out from the acreage just to have lunch or coffee with someone. She doesn't even see her best friend, Suzanne, very often, and except for her, all their comfortable old friends still live in Saskatoon. Gerhardt never relied much on friends anyway, and as the years go by is becoming more unsociable. He seems to find her sufficient, and she supposes she should be thankful he isn't the type to be out all the time with old drinking buddies.

As night falls, she calls him to meet her at the station. She catches the eye of the man across from her as she unfolds her cell phone, but he ignores her and stares out the window. He glances at her again when he hears her speak English, but says nothing. Momentarily steeped in heat, she takes off her jacket and fans herself with the pamphlet from the art gallery.

She thinks of her walk in the beech forest and regrets again that she hasn't brought a sketchbook. But she has never been near to creating anything much more than satisfactory. Mediocre. She was never invited to show her work anywhere and in the end gave up. Which means she isn't an artist at all. She isn't much of anything at all, not a great mother or wife, and only a substitute teacher, a stand-in for a real one.

The man across from her opens his newspaper again and folds it at the crossword puzzle, taking a pen out of his shirt pocket. He looks exactly like someone you'd describe as nondescript: brown suit, brown hair, neither fat nor thin, his eyes carefully expressionless. She feels as if she is his twin.

THREE

Gerhardt is always at his very worst in airports, and she can see that today will be no exception. They managed to get out of Berlin all right, but now in Heathrow, on their way with their carry-ons to the transatlantic flight, they are called to the side because something isn't right. She realizes they've forgotten to place their shampoo and other liquids and gels separately in ziplock bags on top of the luggage. "Sorry," she says to the stern-faced little man in front of her. "We packed them in baggies but forgot to take them out of the suitcases." He nods, holds the bag of hair products, various creams and unguents up against the light, and sends her on her way.

Gerhardt has been sent to another agent down the line. He isn't faring as well. She can tell from the angry set of his back that he is being difficult, making trouble for himself as usual. The middle-aged woman dealing with him is red-faced and annoyed, saying, "It's not our fault you were stopped. There are regulations you must follow, and you haven't complied with them."

Lisa rolls her eyes and settles on a bench to wait as the woman decides to dig deeper through his suitcase. He will never learn. He is always like this, sullen and heavily sarcastic whenever he's asked to open his luggage. And there's still the boarding line-up to look forward to. Last time they flew anywhere—it must have been Mexico—he was incensed at not being at the front of the queue because of her slowness in filling out a form.

When they reach the departure gate, he is still livid. "All that shit because of a couple of bottles of shampoo."

"Gerhardt. If you didn't act like such an asshole she wouldn't have bothered to lecture you. You do this every time." She can see he is already looking around edgily for an opportunity to crash the queue or get into a faster one. Sure enough, he guides her toward a short line-up for priority passengers. She wants to strangle him.

"We are not priority passengers," she points out.

"Never mind," he says. Knowing it is useless to dig in her heels, that it would only create a scene and she'd end up embarrassed, she decides to see what will happen. This time they are lucky. The official, portly, male, and bland, examines their passports and boarding passes and nods them on. He doesn't want a scene either.

··

FLYING ISN'T WHAT it used to be. Air Canada has added so many extra seats to the jet from Heathrow to Calgary that Gerhardt either has to sit doubled up or with his legs sprawled in the aisle, tripping the flight attendants. He of course chooses to sprawl, and Lisa has to stifle a prickle of irritation every time someone has to manoeuvre around him. He decides at one point he's had a bit of leftover trash on his fold-out tray long enough, and he simply gathers it up and thrusts it at a flight attendant passing by. Taken aback, she accepts it automatically, and Lisa closes her eyes. This type of thoughtless discourtesy is so ordinary in their travels it isn't worth commenting on. He wouldn't know what she was talking about.

Oddly, he is much better at home, or anywhere in Canada. She would never catch him treating a waitress in Swift Current or Medicine Hat that way. It's foreign travel that brings out his Mr. Hyde. His German-ness.

What really gets to her is the disdain she senses from other women, especially in airports—other passengers or airline and border officials who obviously think she is some kind of pitiful dishrag, putting up with such a lout. She should have been more observant today, changed places with him so that she ended up with the female customs officer. His attitude, especially with his German accent, almost always brings out in these women a desire to punish. He has been ignored, yelled at, called aside and left to wait, treated with contempt in so many airports that now when-ever they have to deal with a female official, he will usually stand quietly while Lisa acquires boarding passes, displays visas, and answers questions about their destination. Even then she senses him being scrutinized, feels as if she is trying to pass a rottweiler off as a golden retriever.

She'd love to go somewhere with someone else, travel once again in the company of that patient Canadian smugness, that way of tolerating the irritations of travel with the dry condescen-sion she used to find so annoying in Canadian men. Or to travel on her own, sense of direction or not.

Now she stares out, past the young woman beside her reading a romance novel, at the golden sheen of the sun on cotton-batten clouds. It isn't only middle age that makes him difficult and bull-headed. He's been like this from the beginning, and she put up with it right from the first few weeks they were together. In the end, maybe all those women in airports are right: she is a dishrag.

That first visit to Europe after Stephanie was born, by the Baltic Sea, changing her diaper on the beach. His anger, his disgust at

Lisa for getting sand on her face. Packing up their things in an absolute fury for the long drive back to the city. Such needless hurt over nothing, such harsh undermining of her sureness.

Or on the same trip, when he was in another rage over something she can't recall, and she, trying to keep up with him, tripped and fell out of the subway in Berlin. He walked on, pushing the stroller, and called back, "I suppose that was my fault too?" She was ready to leave him after that trip. But safely at home again and not eager to be a single parent, she let him talk her out of it.

Part of her problem now is that she has such a good memory. She fans herself with the in-flight magazine. Here she is still stewing over bad behaviour long past, and for what? If she were going to leave, she should have done it years ago. She scrutinizes him now, dozing beside her.

He wakes with a start, and takes off the airline headphones. He examines her expression, and says, "Maybe when you go into town on Saturdays you could see that naturopath Suzanne was talking about."

She knows he is encouraging her to do something about hot flashes and other unspecific symptoms because it would improve his own quality of life. He recently showed her a magazine article and two websites he found on the benefits of hormone-replacement therapy, in spite of the new study claiming it to be dangerous. She makes a noncommittal noise and opens the magazine. The pilot announces they are experiencing some turbulence and Gerhardt puts on his seatbelt (she hadn't taken hers off in the first place), and takes her hand, knowing bumpy rides make her nervous.

··

AT HOME the next morning, she is up with jet lag at 4 a.m., surfing the internet. The house is cool and silent except for the exhausted echoes of Gerhardt's snoring. She checks her email. Nothing but those she's already read, one from Suzanne welcoming her back, and one from Tyler, with no mention of why he hadn't shown up to visit them and his grandparents. He and Céline are now in Bulgaria. Bulgaria? Why on earth would they want to go there? But then again, why not? They are young and free, able to go wherever fate leads them.

Fate, she thinks, led her to the Max Ernst retrospective. She googles "Ernst asparagus," wondering just how many of them are out there. A little garden of lunar ones, perhaps others: a solar asparagus; a twilight one; asparagi dancing at dawn. But no. All that shows up on the screen is the statue she saw five days ago, apparently for the second time, and that's it. The only one in the world. Her asparagus doesn't exist. She zooms in on the computer image, and here too, this vacant lump of a head with a hollowed-out recess of a mouth holds no joy for her whatsoever.

In New York it existed as something entirely different. Maybe it is the city itself, its influence on her. She once heard someone say New York is like Mexico City in that you either love or hate it. She fell for both New York and Mexico City. For Berlin as well, in fact. Maybe she would like all huge cities, the vastness of their energy, the hum of humanity and traffic, that intangible tension that wouldn't leave her psyche until she found herself home again, caught in a silence so profound it seemed dangerous.

Gerhardt liked *Lunar Asparagus* too, so much so that he'd asked the MoMA store if there was a poster of it, but they didn't have one. She has to admit he can be genial and fun to be with, even while travelling—pleasant with strangers, courteous to old ladies. Elderly women like her Aunt Gemma, in fact, often fall for him at first sight. In their first apartment in Saskatoon, a pillar-legged old farm widow living a floor above them thought he was God's gift.

When they rode the elevator together, Gerhardt could make gentle, charming conversation with her while Lisa looked at the floor numbers. Once, when she and Lisa were alone, the woman eyed her, tying her flower-patterned scarf under her chin, and said, "You don't know what a good man you've got there."

"Oh yes I do," Lisa told her, rather jocularly. The next time they encountered her in the elevator, the woman paid no attention to Gerhardt but asked Lisa if she would come over and cut her toe-nails. She tries to recall what she could possibly have replied.

All her aunts, her dad's sisters included, were smitten, reflecting back at him the glow of a courtly European presence he never seemed to show for anyone younger. And although she never quite reached the category of old lady, her mother had loved him from the first day Lisa brought him home and he, as a prospective German son-in-law, presented her with the traditional bouquet of flowers.

She tries Google again, types "series of asparagus," and this time gets nothing but recipes. She should try to get a few hours' sleep. But her body contains that zinging sensation, not vibrating exactly, but far too awake. Wanting to recapture some of the cathedral stillness of the German woods, she thinks of searching for *Buchenwald*, but of course she'd be offered websites she has no desire to see. She types in "beech forest." Besides various resorts and parks, a site on tree planting in Bulgaria comes up. Where Tyler and Céline are. Tyler's email, as usual, isn't very informative: "Got to Bulgaria, staying with friends in Sofia. Having a great time, will write more later." Later has yet to come. It's Céline's influence. She's turned Tyler into a vegetarian, so now he never has enough energy even to write long emails.

But of course she is being silly. Tyler has strength and stamina in all kinds of ways, and a generous sense of humour. Wiry and not as tall as his father, he has Gerhardt's smile and her father's blue, almond-shaped eyes and hawkish nose and her own springy brown hair. He was a long-distance runner in high school, and is still able to run, fast and steady, for miles. He has always been clear-eyed and observant, able to think problems through, to calmly consider obstacles without any drama no matter how long it takes. She is very proud of him and wonders now if he knows that.

Once when he was three years old, Gerhardt was taking him somewhere in the car. He yelled, "Goodbye, Mom!" and she got to the door just in time to see him run jauntily down the walk in his cowboy hat, enough of a toddler yet to have a hint of hope in his voice as he said, with a loud, teasing question mark, "It's my turn to drive, right Dad?" Even now she can feel that enervating surge, like an electric current, making her so weak with love she had to sit down on the steps to wave goodbye. She feels a ridiculous pang of grief. Her little boy is gone now, existing only in the past.

The snoring from the bedroom is gone. Maybe if she tries lying down, she can force herself to sleep. But no. A clatter in the kitchen indicates Gerhardt is up, making coffee. Just what she needs, a jolt of caffeine. But then again, it is morning; maybe she should force herself to stay awake until evening and get up at a reasonable time tomorrow. He slouches into the office, eyes the computer screen, and massages the back of her neck. "Do you want coffee?"

She lets her head droop. "No. Oh well, yes, maybe I will have some. Did you get any sleep?"

"No. I dozed for a few minutes."

"You were snoring a lot longer than that." He ignores this and wanders back into the kitchen. She checks her email. No new messages.

THE YARD AND GARDEN are strewn with yellow and brown leaves and most of the flowers are dead as there have been a couple of hard frosts already. She wonders if she should suggest planning a trip south in January, even though two trips with Gerhardt in one year might prove disastrous. She's finishing her second cup of coffee and contemplating all the raking she has to do when the superintendent of the Northern school district phones. A week ago she put her name in at the rural district as well as the city, thinking she'd try to work regularly, contribute more to household expenses, keep busy. Shit. She looks at the call display. It's 8:45 in the morning. A teacher must have phoned in sick at the last minute and now she'll be expected to drive to some Elk Armpit or other in twenty minutes. Except why wouldn't the principal of whichever school it was be calling? She answers the phone.

"Good morning!" Al Forchuck has a booming voice so hearty she finds it always induces a slight sense of doom.

"Hello, Al." She tries to seem friendly if not cheerful.

After some chit-chat, he gets to the point. "Yeah, so Lisa, I'm not phoning about a job for you. I've got a proposition for Ger. Is he around?"

Ger. She gives him Gerhardt's office number.

..

"SO WHAT was Al phoning about today?" They are at the kitchen counter making sandwiches to eat in front of the TV.

"They want to hire me to set up new computers in Caribou Point and then run training classes for the teaching staff and the community." Gerhardt opens a pickle jar, giving her an oblique look. "I'd fly up there this month and be staying till Christmas."

"Really! Are you going?" She tries to look neutral. Over two months. The prospect of being single opens before her, a clear vista rainbowed with small indulgences: reading all day without having to cook supper; drinking too much wine and playing Scrabble with Suzanne. Suzanne could even take a day or two off work, visit for days on end maybe.

She and Suzanne have been friends since they were students, sharing apartments, music, clothes, recreational drugs, everything except boyfriends, and those were sometimes hard to tell apart. They'd gone to Mexico and the States together, hitchhiked around Canada, settled in Saskatoon, and seen each other through finding jobs, raising kids, marriage crises. It was only because Suzanne moved to Prince Albert that Gerhardt was able to talk Lisa into leaving Saskatoon and buying an acreage in the area. And since they moved here, Suzanne has been her main social contact, which is fine—all she needs or wants really is one good friend.

"Yes, I think I'll take them up on it," Gerhardt says. "They pay very well. Maybe we can then take a trip next winter."

Caribou Point. She went up there once to help Suzanne do a workshop on adapting curriculums. It's a northern reserve you have to fly into, a treeless lakeside village in the midst of scrub forest. From the air it looks like a kid's diorama, its faded prefab bungalows sitting like painted shoeboxes beside a mirror. "Two months is a long time," she says. She would continue to accept the odd job to keep her grounded in the real world but would be grateful to work only part time. "Maybe instead of a trip we can get new shingles." She meets his eyes, mildly confrontational. His shoulders stiffen with stubbornness as he turns toward the counter to add condiments to his sandwich. Since their initial improvements to the house and acreage, getting Gerhardt to okay any more work has been nearly impossible. Too bad it's almost winter or she'd just go ahead and hire somebody to do the roof while he is away. Never mind. She pokes him in the ribs. "Don't waste time sulking. You'll likely be gone soon."

"You started it." But he sets his sandwich down and puts his arms around her. When she kisses him, his mouth tastes of mustard.

By the end of the week, he's had a lunch meeting with Al in Prince Albert, signed a contract, and bought canned groceries and Ichiban soup in bulk to take up north with him. The computers have already been shipped on the barge.

She gives up trying to pack groceries in the few boxes he is allowed to take on the plane when he keeps unpacking the ones she is doing. "Here," he says. "Like this."

She shakes her head, gives up, and pours herself a drink. Noticing him slide a bottle of vodka between packets of soup, she says primly, "Caribou Point is a dry reserve, you know."

"Don't worry, with one bottle for two months I won't be throwing any parties."

At the end of the week, she drives Gerhardt, his suitcase, and his cartons to the airport, and finds herself alone.

FOUR

D riving into Prince Albert on her way to Suzanne's for lunch, Lisa feels weighed down, not just by her parka, but oppressed. Car exhaust hangs in icy clouds. She can't set foot outside without feeling attacked, bitten by frost. Why on earth, back when she and Gerhardt were young and had the choice of living anywhere on this planet, had they been stupid enough to choose her home province? Germany had never appealed to either of them, but somewhere like New Zealand or Australia?

She turns right on a red light, spinning her wheels to get through a drift that the city hasn't plowed yet. She could be driving comfortably down a warm street in a suburb of Sydney or Canberra, looking forward to a barbecue. With someone other than Suzanne, of course. There was that. She should be thankful to be here, able to visit her oldest and dearest friend whenever she wants.

As in the Leonard Cohen song, Suzanne's condo is down near the river. Although she is now well past shopping at Salvation Army counters, after lunch she does serve tea, and her coffee table features a bowl of mandarins. Suzanne is still quite slender, with dark blonde hair that has a natural streak of platinum and no grey yet. Her hair used to be spectacular when she was young and grew it long. Now she wears it in a grown-out bob similar to Lisa's.

"I really hate when it gets so cold in November and we're still not used to it," Suzanne says. "I'm glad I didn't have to work today."

"Speaking of work, I'm trying to be available for more hours. We need the money after our trip."

They chat on in the desultory manner of old friends who don't require each other to be interesting.

"Any news of Hancock the Horrible lately?" Lisa asks, and immediately regrets bringing up the subject. Hank, Suzanne's second ex-husband, is regularly spotted downtown with different, always younger girlfriends.

Suzanne pours the tea from a handmade pot, slopping on the glass coffee table and not bothering to wipe it up. "The news is, I've finally given up caring," she says.

"Good," Lisa says. Maybe that is true at last. Considering she's wearing a pair of sweatpants and no makeup, Suzanne is looking better today than she has for a while, maybe even since her divorce. Finding out about Hank's infidelities had been devastating for her. Still, in spite of despising Hank, Lisa rather misses him. For one thing, now that he is gone, Gerhardt prefers to let the two women socialize on their own. "I feel like a third wheel now," he told her.

"Fifth wheel," she corrected automatically.

"But there's just three of us."

"Yes, but that's not the way the saying goes."

"It could be about bicycles. I'd be the third wheel on a bike."

"Then it would be a tricycle. The simile wouldn't hold up." They often have stupid arguments about English expressions to absolutely no purpose, as if Gerhardt could change her mind about her native language.

Hank and Gerhardt were never real friends, but they both made a good-natured effort to get along so that the two women didn't have to worry about dragging them to each other's dinners. And Lisa appreciated Hank's sense of humour. With Hank, she didn't have to roll her eyes and explain puns as she does with Gerhardt, or sometimes Suzanne for that matter. Although now that she thinks about it, she was always aware that she got on Hank's nerves by laughing at her own jokes, or by making silly observations after too much wine. Really, she'd liked Suzanne's first husband, Charles, better, although he wasn't as entertaining. Or as good-looking. Unlike Charles, who'd turned pudgy in his thirties, Hank was lean from working out in the gym, and handsome in a too-polished way. She never felt any vibes of attraction, either for or from him, which was of course a good thing. He seemed interested only in Suzanne, and the fact that this turned out not to be true still mystifies Lisa.

Sipping tea in comfortable silence, they stare out the window beyond the fifth-floor balcony at the new snowdrifts shovelled beside the sidewalk, the bleak expanse of the Saskatchewan River flashing an occasional glimpse of tarnished silver against the snow. "I was talking on the phone to Lynne yesterday," Suzanne says. "She was wondering how Stephanie's doing." Her expression sharpens with sympathy. "I told her I didn't know, but that she was in B.C."

"She's still in Nelson with Kelvin, whoever he is, and working in a bar. We don't talk very often, but she seems to be doing better, at least holding down a job, so maybe he's a good influence. Whatever she's doing, the sad thing is I'm way happier now that she's not around."

In the years before Stephanie's move to B.C., she would intermittently come home to borrow money, sometimes staying days or weeks, sleeping off narcotics or mania or who knew what, coming and going with friends who would show up in the yard honking their horns. The last time she turned up wired and exhausted, whining and sullen, her lovely eyes hollow with sly desperation, they insisted once again on rehab. But she checked herself out of detox in P.A. within a week and went back to Saskatoon, maxing out a credit card Lisa didn't often use and had left drawing attention to itself in a drawer. Despair sometimes makes her want to wail like a Muslim mother on the news, to drop to her knees and strike her forehead on the floor. But that's just stupid. At least Stephanie is alive.

"And Tyler?" Suzanne brightens, knowing Tyler is usually good news.

"Fine, I guess. But they never did show up in Germany. You know Céline. She thinks we're ecologically corrupt philistines and doesn't want to have much to do with us. I just wish he was with someone more suitable. Well, I might as well say it: someone better." Perpetually un- or underemployed, Céline is plain and humourless, playing up her eco-nerdy look with dark-framed glasses and goofy hand-woven hats. Lisa pictures Gerhardt's parents' expressions if they'd had the opportunity to meet her; maybe it's just as well she and Tyler hadn't turned up. "And I worry about him living with somebody so morally sure of herself." She wonders how Céline gets on with her own parents, the Jenkinses, who after all named her after Céline Dion.

"Tyler's still young," Suzanne says. "He could easily split up with Céline and find his ideal partner." She makes a face. "As if there were such a thing."

"I don't worry too much about him. I know he's a sensible kid. And at least he has a degree, even if it is in sociology. Anyway, it's not as if Céline is a terrible person or anything." Tyler would land on his feet no matter what happened. Lisa has confidence, has always had confidence ever since he was a curious, observant, casually eccentric little boy, that he would do well, and so far she has been right. She is about to ask how Lynne is but can see Suzanne is about to reveal something.

"You know, I was going to mention this during lunch, but then…"

"Well, what?"

"I've been making some plans. I have to go to Ontario in a couple of weeks. My sister's there now, arranging for Dad to go into a home."

"What's your mom going to do?"

"When I get there, I'm supposed to deal with getting her into the same home, different care level. She doesn't want to go, and she's still got her marbles. Donna has to go back to Halifax and is leaving all that to me. Plus, I'll have to do something about the house."

"God. Sometimes I think my parents did me a favour, dying in their sixties."

Suzanne ignores this. "I'm taking early retirement. I've put in enough years in education. I'll do pretty well."

"Oh, that's great, Suzanne! If you don't have to work, you can come out to our place whenever you want, stay for a week at a time. Next summer we can go for walks down the Métis trail and drive out to the lake. God, you've been so busy you haven't even been out to see me since Gerhardt left." She pictures long afternoons, the two of them drinking wine on their deck. Maybe that's just what she needs, a woman friend around more often.

"The thing is…" Suzanne looks down. "I've more or less made up my mind that I'll move to Guelph. Or at least I'll try it for a while. Then my mom can take her time deciding what to do. We'll see first how it goes with me there."

"Suzanne!" Lisa is so shocked she feels shot with novocaine. "That's a terrible idea. What will I do without you?"

"You'll survive, I guess, like I will. I just feel that because of Mom's bad heart, I can't leave her on her own, even in a care home.

Donna still has her job, her husband and kids in Halifax. She can't take much time off."

"Your mom is ill, Suzanne. You're not a nurse."

"She likely doesn't have too much time left. I could have Home Care in. I could make her last year or two happier. And of course, Lynne's in Toronto. I would be near her. I think she has finally forgiven me for leaving her father." Suzanne left Charles for Hank more than a decade ago. Lynne, at eighteen, took her father's side.

"Well, I can't think of any good arguments against you moving, except it will make me very sad."

"I know. I wish we'd spent more time together after you moved here. And we could have gone on a couple of trips or something. We always had such good times, travelling." Suzanne pours the last of the tea. "I wish I'd gone with you to Europe instead of spending all that time in Mexico with Charles. I've hardly been anywhere since."

"I wish you'd gone with me too. I'd have had more fun with you than I did with Maureen. Travelling with you was kind of like being alone."

Suzanne laughs. "Thanks a lot."

"Well, you know what I mean. You always made me feel as free as if I were by myself, and we always made decisions together. Maureen got on my nerves. She liked to have her own way, and she was always striking up conversations with other travellers for no good reason. And she insisted on a certain level of alertness and competency, not like you and me drifting along. After we broke up in Barcelona, I felt almost euphoric at finding myself alone."

"You always liked Maureen, though. You got along really well when you worked together."

"Oh yes, and we did fine all through England and France. We agreed about where to go and what to do when we got there, shared traveller's cheques and all that. But then she sort of naturally fell into being the leader, not only in decision-making, but literally, always forging ahead in the right direction. It was like travelling with a man, without the fringe benefits."

"Huh. Men are irritating even with the fringe benefits."

"In Spain, I finally told her I was tired of trailing after her and that I wanted to go back to London by myself, earn enough money to spend an entire year in Europe. I liked Europe, and I wanted to see more of it than Maureen's back. Also, it was January, too cold to camp out anymore even by the Mediterranean. I wanted to sit out the winter in a cozy pub with English speakers."

"Was she very upset? I would be, suddenly informed I had to be on my own."

"I've never really thought about it that way; she was always the competent one." It occurs to Lisa that besides Suzanne, she has never travelled for any length of time with anyone other than Maureen and Gerhardt, both of whom she considers difficult. Maybe she is the one who is difficult. Maybe Suzanne is unusually patient and good-natured. "Yes, it was a pretty awful thing to do, I guess. She was upset, but we went to one of the bars near the campground and bought a jug of red wine. We eventually decided it was better to split up while we were still friends. Well, I've told you all this before, Suzanne."

Suzanne shakes her head. "Not really, or not in any detail. Maybe you did years ago, but I can't remember."

"Anyway, Maureen went to Morocco with a vanload of Swedes, and I caught a ride to Calais with a couple of gay bartenders from B.C. who'd parked their van next to our tent. I remember finding it interesting that all the heavy breathing and grunting when you have sex sounds the same no matter what."

"Remember when we were camping with Mary and Owen? Outside Banff?"

"Yes!" Lisa laughs, recalling noisy friends. "The bartenders were fun to travel with. They liked to sing old Canadian standards: "Farewell to Nova Scotia," that sort of thing. They even knew "Men of the Royal Mounted." We cruised through French villages belting it out for the *gendarmes* until they dropped me off at the hovercraft to Dover and I met an American girl from Oregon looking for someone to hitchhike with her to London. She was on her way back to the States, cutting it so close that when we got to the city she went straight to Heathrow. I checked in at a place called O'Callaghan's Nightly Tourist Accommodations. I don't remember how I found it. Really, it was nothing but a collection of cubicles with beds taking up any space available. That same night I met a group of Australians who were looking for an extra person to share a house they'd just rented in Shepherd's Bush. So that was that. I was all set for a winter in London."

Finishing her tea, she says, "If I hadn't split up with Maureen, I'd never have stayed long enough to go to Greece or Israel."

"You'd never have met Gerhardt."

"God. Just imagine." A life without Gerhardt. All that space he took up: what, or whom, would she have filled it with? "I always ended up falling in with other people, I don't even recall how it happened."

Suzanne adds more honey to her tea. "You were young. And it was the times. Peace and love, all that. Do you ever hear anything from Maureen?"

"No, we lost touch after she moved to Vancouver in the eighties." She scrutinizes Suzanne as if taking her picture while she's still here right across from her, gazing out her window at the Saskatchewan winter with a dreamy, preoccupied look. All the ways she hasn't changed over the years.

"And here I am, old enough to retire no matter where I decide to live," Suzanne says. "Maybe I'll eventually take a trip to Europe, see what I missed. Of course, that would be entirely different from going there as a twenty-year-old."

Lisa nods. "Maybe we can take a trip together one day. Although you would have to put up with Gerhardt. Actually, that might work out well, having someone along to help stifle him. His Germanity."

Suzanne grins but doesn't comment.

"It will likely do you good to get away from here altogether, Hank and all that. Not that I'm encouraging you to move away. Really, I'm not joking, Suzanne. I really don't know what I'll do without you."

"We'll email. We'll visit. I might move back here after my parents...uh..." She sits up straight, looking determinedly positive. "Anyway, right now we have to get together again before I go. I'll come out this weekend."

The real prospect of Suzanne's absence now produces a knot in the pit of Lisa's stomach. They would keep in touch, but it wouldn't be the same. Without Suzanne, socializing will become a branch of her life entirely bare. And just when Gerhardt is gone too.

They continue to visit, just comfortably chatting, really, until it's almost dusk. As Lisa puts on her boots and coat and says her goodbyes, she tells herself not to get weepy. Of course Suzanne wants to be in Guelph with her parents, especially with Lynne close by. What she said about her own parents doing her a favour by dying in their sixties was a joke. Their deaths, both of cancer a couple of years apart, can still strike her with an orphan's grief, even though she was able to take off all the time she needed when each of them was ill. Youth fades, parents die, daughters break your heart, friends leave you. It's all just life, going on.

FIVE

B y the time she gets home, it's dark, and she forgot to turn the yard light on. She fumbles the key into the lock and as she turns on the light, wonders what to make for supper. Scrounging in the fridge for eggs and cheese, she sees the bottle of Pinot Grigio chilling in the door and realizes what she really needs is a drink. She should have asked Suzanne if she could stay overnight. They could have drunk a bottle or two of wine together, softened the news of her impending departure. As she pours her glass of wine, she hopes Suzanne really can make it for a visit before she leaves. She'll be busy wrapping things up at work and making arrangements for her condo. Will she leave it empty until she decides what to do with it? For a split second, she thinks Suzanne could ask Gerhardt to look in on it now and then on his way home from the office. But of course he is gone too.

It isn't as if this is the first time Gerhardt's work has taken him away, but those earlier contracts never lasted longer than two weeks. Contemplating this new-found expanse of time without either him or Suzanne, she begins to acquire a sense of aimless dread, as if she were the only passenger on a boat that has lost its anchor.

She walks around the empty house, sipping her wine, turning up the heat. Although she isn't making a sound, there seems to be an echo. "All by Myself," a song she doesn't like, runs through her head. She turns on the radio to the French station that plays jazz at this hour and ramps the sound up for Ella Fitzgerald.

Preparing to whip up an omelet, she sees she'll soon have to shop for groceries. She should have done that today while she had the car out. After a quick meal at the kitchen table, she calls Suzanne. "I just wanted to let you know I got home all right. I'm having a second glass of wine here and thought jeez, I should have stayed overnight. We could have had a few drinks and mulled things over."

"Aw. Yes, especially since it's Sunday tomorrow. I didn't even think of drinks. I should have invited you, but my mind is so cluttered lately."

"I could have invited myself but it didn't occur to me. I just thought, well I had to drive so…"

"But I'll come for sure next weekend, for a couple of days."

"You'd better." She should offer help, now that Suzanne is getting ready to leave, but can't think of anything she could actually do. Packing is personal, the main effort choosing what to bring, and of course she can't help her out with her last days at work.

She sits with the phone in her hand. She loves Suzanne. She is always so comfortable around her, can always say anything that comes into her head and Suzanne will listen. Listen and approve, no matter what, a deep approval of everything she is, even when they disagree. And she feels the same way about Suzanne. Admiration of Suzanne's judgement and character has helped form her own; her friend is a weathervane she can always trust to point in the right direction. Suzanne has heard all her stories but never minds hearing them again; she isn't being merely indulgent, although that's part of it. She is genuinely interested. They both get animated with reminiscence.

The fluorescent kitchen lights seem suddenly too bright, making the room and the smudged white fridge and stove too large and spartan. She is hit again with nostalgia, recalling the kitchen she shared with the Australians in London. It was dimly lit and almost always full of warm human beings. She was able to appreciate the hominess without having to contribute to it, could reheat her fish and chips in the midst of five other people while the latest excitement wafted over her like the smell of home baking.

Living with the Australians had been fun. They were homogenously good-natured and boisterous, calling each other prawns and lamenting London's lack of Vegemite. They assumed her to be different, and allowed her to mind her own business even though they infringed relentlessly on one another's privacy, expecting sympathy and advice regarding the sometimes melodramatic business of their own lives. Instead of feeling out of place, she was happy. She was delighted with everything until it occurred to her she'd better find a job.

Even that enterprise turned out to be relatively easy. One of the Australians worked off and on as a temporary office worker, and simply asked the supervisor at the agency if Lisa could come in for a typing test. A couple of days later, she was sent on her first job: five days of typing invoices at O.E. Nunn and Co., on Neal Street.

It wasn't all wonderful, of course. The corduroy jacket and light sweater she'd thought would have to do for workwear did little to warm the morning walk to Shepherd's Bush tube station, and once she got there, underground seemed as cold as outside. She felt as if she were descending into an Orwellian purgatory. The Londoners going to work looked peaked and unhealthy, their pale faces and bad teeth leaving a general impression of malaise that seemed to drift somewhere between her shoulder blades, making her want to hunch forward.

Considering her usual sense of direction, she'd been pleased at how easy it was to navigate the streets of London and the Underground. She found the address on Neal Street with no problem. It was an old Victorian building, and she had to climb two flights of dark wooden stairs varnished to a dangerous shine before she came to the little suite of rooms that contained O.E. Nunn and Co. She was greeted, somewhat curtly at first, by a thin man in a brown tweed suit with a North Country accent and horn-rimmed glasses. He introduced himself as Mr. Wilkes and, pointing to a stack of handwritten invoices by a dusty manual typewriter, said, "You'll have your work cut out for you." He indicated the carbon sheets beside the typing paper. "We need two copies of each one. Best get down to business." He nodded at the closed door of a small office and said, "You'll meet my partner, Mr. Greenly, when we have tea at ten or thereabouts."

Lisa wondered where O.E. Nunn could be. Rolling layers of paper and carbon into the typewriter, trying not to smudge her fingers, she thought of Maureen sauntering through the spicy marketplaces of Marrakech and looked at her watch. Eight hours.

Seeing that she knew what she was doing, Mr. Wilkes said, "Right. There you are, then, and I'll chat with you later." He disappeared around a corner.

Everything in the office was made of wood, the doors and door frames highly polished, her desk worn and scratched like the floor. Even the walls were wood-panelled. The floor featured an area rug that at one time might have contained some red but was now a nondescript rust colour, as if it were something growing in a hollow log. Winnie the Pooh's house. She noticed the tea things set out, ready for ten o'clock. She'd better start making typing noises, she thought, and separated another invoice from the messy pile.

By working steadily and putting her watch away in a drawer, she managed to make it to tea break. Mr. Wilkes plugged in the kettle a few minutes early, and at ten exactly, Mr. Greenly emerged. He was a round, genial-looking man, who said "How do you do" when Mr. Wilkes introduced him, then ducked back into his office with his cup of tea and closed the door.

Mr. Wilkes arranged himself on the wooden chair beside the tea table and chatted comfortably with her about the weather, how she liked London, who would win the next election. His curtness, she realized, was not at all unfriendly; it was just his manner.

"I understand Canadians are offended if one mistakes them for Americans," he said. "I for one can never tell the difference."

Refusing to rise to the bait, if that's what it was, she agreed that no European should be expected to tell the difference, and what's more, who cared? In fact, she found most Canadians to be smug to the point of imbecility with their stupid maple leaves plastered to their backpacks, expecting everybody to love them, and she told him so.

By her third day of working for him, he was telling stories about his family and showing her snapshots of the land he owned in Wales. He and his wife hoped to retire there and build a cottage. She told him about northern Saskatchewan and the cabin her mother's sister Gemma and her husband Max owned near La Ronge. Her aunt and uncle had grown sons by the time she started school, and they liked children, Lisa in particular, she told him, so she'd vacationed with them for two weeks every summer from age eight to sixteen. Twice she'd brought a friend along, but she really preferred to go alone. She read books or sketched scenery when she wasn't swimming or exploring the bush.

She pours herself another glass of wine, feeling a bit sentimental about her time in the North. The tang of evergreens in the air, the crunch of caribou moss and Labrador tea under her feet. She loved all of it, the clear water hemmed by spruce and birch trees growing out of moss and sheer rock, the giant flat stone where she could sunbathe and from which she could dive into the lake. She loved her aunt and uncle, who aside from teaching her to fish and pick berries, never demanded a thing except that she enjoy her holiday. Just last year she attended Max's funeral in Regina. Aunt Gemma is still living, if that is what you call it, in a seniors' home in the city.

La Ronge is part of the rugged beauty of the Precambrian Shield country, she told Mr. Wilkes. She described for him her little bedroom that held pine bunk beds, the log walls and floor, the framed carved relief of an elk, everything of wood. "A bit like this office," she said, looking around. The morning tea break that day lasted so long Mr. Greenly peered out of his doorway, curious and benign, while she and Mr. Wilkes smoked Benson & Hedges and waxed eloquent, as Mr. Wilkes put it, about their respective north countries.

Wrapping a long scarf around his neck, Mr. Greenly announced that he was feeling a bit under the weather, needed to go for a walk around the block for some fresh air. Mr. Wilkes said walking in London for fresh air was like going underground when you needed light. He longed, he said, to hike against the winds on the wild heaths of Wales.

Lisa tried to picture Mr. Wilkes with his narrow shoulders and defeated-looking neck set against the wild winds of Wales. She looked sadly at her watch and saw it was time to get back to her dwindling pile of invoices.

On her way home that evening, she stopped to listen to some buskers in the tube station sing "Twa Corbies" in a haunting Celtic melody. She remembered the poem from school, by Anonymous. She was reminded of another poem she'd studied, by Tennyson, about the South being seductive and full of betrayal and the North being harsh but true. She decided to ask Mr. Wilkes if he'd heard of it.

On her last day of work, he told her about an unarmed prisoner of war he'd shot during the war. "I killed a man once," he said.

"I beg your pardon?" she asked, and he told his story.

She was hired for a few weeks' typing with Barclay's Bank and intended to stop by O.E. Nunn's some afternoon for a cup of tea but never got around to it. Even now, thirty years later, she feels a pang of guilt because she didn't see Mr. Wilkes again. His story had nothing to do with it. It's just that he was already, even before she left London, someone from her past. She knew people did things in war that would never occur to them in peacetime. Anyway, she decided, in her twenty-three-year-old wisdom, he wasn't the same person he'd been back then. He was quite old, in his mid-fifties at least.

In the spring, she took off for Greece on the Sunshine Bus, one of a fleet of old school buses an enterprising hippie had repainted in psychedelics to drive young people south. In the middle of a rural Yugoslavian road, a young man sauntered up the bus stairs, taking his time. She knew he was French even before he said anything. He sat down beside her, though he had to pass three empty seats to get there. She remembers him making fun of her high school French and wonders now why she let herself be charmed by a short, delicately built aesthete, the opposite of the usual type of man (or boy, she thinks now) she fell for. Certainly the opposite of Gerhardt. It was partly because he was there, so obviously available, and she'd always found it hard to resist someone who found her attractive. She and René lasted long enough to travel to

Ios together, where they grew bored with the beach and nightclub scene and decided, after meeting a couple who'd just come from there and had all the information they needed, to go to Israel. But soon after their plans were made, they both realized it wasn't so much that they were bored with the island but with each other, and after a night of tiresome but oddly friendly airing of complaints, she was relieved once again to find herself on her own.

SIX

She puts on her boots and parka and steps out into a yard covered in powdery layers of snow, but slogs on, determined to get some exercise. She follows a cow path in the bush up to the gravel road, past Danielsons' dugout and down again to hike the old wagon trail that circles back to her house. A small stand of poplars, aspens that have all warped in the same way, expose witches' arms against a grey sky. A stunted white birch struggles to survive against a background of pine, poplar branches, and tangled undergrowth. Up in La Ronge, birches are the main deciduous tree, leaves turning gold every autumn among the evergreens. She tries to picture somewhere in the world where there might be birch forests. In Russia, probably. Didn't Russian novels portray their Natashas and Sonjas moving households to summer dachas that smelled of clean wood and candle wax, serenely sheltered by birch trees?

Days pass. She can't settle in to anything, can't concentrate to read or plan her garden, can't bring herself even to sweep the floor. The peace and quiet she so desired is more and more burdensome, the solitude an imposition, not the escape she was expecting.

Her supply of wine has been quickly depleted and she is well into the leftover gin and scotch, the special-occasion brandy and duty-free tequila. She'll have to go to the liquor store next time she is in P.A. for groceries. Usually Gerhardt does the liquor and grocery shopping.

For days now, the only music she can listen to is *Getz/Gilberto*, the comfortable wail of Stan Getz's saxophone with Joao Gilberto's rough-edged purring: she feels as if no other music exists.

But now she switches off the stereo, the music finally getting on her nerves. She wishes she'd never read Stan Getz's biography. How can she continue to be so enamoured with the music of a drug-addled wife beater? She turns on the TV, which she would never ordinarily watch before supper, and stops channel surfing at a comedy series featuring young men with nothing better to do than hurt themselves skateboarding or doing tricks on motor bikes.

Male wit though the ages. One caveman clubbing another. Don Quixote perpetually getting his head cracked, left at the side of the road with broken limbs, face bashed in and bloody. *Nyuck, nyuck.* Such a classic. She turns the TV off and searches the cupboard for something else to drink.

··

THAT NIGHT, Gerhardt phones. She tries to sound cheerful. "Are you still slaving away at the school so late in the evening?"

"I live here now."

"What?" In October they had a house for him, but with no phone or internet.

"Some teachers needed the house and they moved me to a tourist cabin." He has that quality in his voice she knows so well, that amused disgust, as if he'd expected nothing better, and as usual, it had come to pass. "It was, you could say, rustic. It's thirty below here at night and the heater was faulty. When it did warm up a little, it reincarnated about a million flies. So I just asked a student with a half-ton to help me move the bed to an empty office in the school."

Had he asked anyone for permission to do that? She doubts it. "Are you quitting then? Coming home?"

"Ach, no. It's not ideal, but I use the home ec kitchen and there's showers and whatnot. And it's free." He goes on to talk about his students, the teachers he has sessions with after school, and a group from the community he is teaching. Several of them miss class regularly. "They have two excuses," he says. "Babysitter doesn't show up, or they have to get wood. So I thought I'd see what a big deal this wood-getting was, that it should take up a whole day. I said I wanted to help out on the weekend. So Sol Beavereye came over last Saturday and said they were on their way to borrow a truck, and I could come with." He recounts a sad, convoluted comedy about the search for enough gas for the truck, then plowing their way through back roads in the bush, stuck in deep snow several times and having to shovel, finally finding a stand of deadwood in snow piled so high they had to work like hell the rest of the day just to harvest enough for a couple of households for a week.

"My god," she says. "And you did this just to see how bad a pretext it was."

"Yes." He pauses. "So I'll never question that excuse again." His voice holds a zest she hasn't heard in a while. He is getting a charge out of all of it, having an adventure. He would finish the contract.

She misses him. She misses his voice, his jokes that sometimes are stupid and sometimes just fit. One afternoon years ago in Saskatoon when the kids were in school, the day before the delivery of a new bed, he'd called her name and she trudged up the stairs, mildly irritated, and there he was lying nude on the mattress with a bottle of champagne and fifteen roses, as many years as they'd had the bed, ready to celebrate its demise and see it off properly. She grins, recalling another argument about language. "It's a hard-*on*," she had to insist, although not able to come up with a reason, "not hard *one*."

She met Gerhardt, strangely enough, on a kibbutz in Israel. After her affair with René and his gentle insinuating chauvinism had ended in Greece, she decided to take the side trip they'd been planning anyway, to work as a foreign volunteer near Haifa. So she booked a cheap flight to Israel, partly because she had all the information about the kibbutz in which they'd planned on staying and partly because she was running low on money and knew she could live there free for up to a year. And really, she'd wanted to see Israel for a long time. She wasn't sure why. Maybe in the small-town Saskatchewan world of her childhood, Israel embodied all that was exotic. All those Bible stories, those Sunday school pictures of Jesus riding a donkey, palm branches spread luxuriantly on the street in front of him, buildings plastered in clay the colour of the surrounding hills, the great barred gate to Jerusalem open in welcome.

Gerhardt, in the midst of his own travels, had taken up with an English girl, one of those well-groomed British hippies who still looked perfect after weeks of camping and youth hostels, her Indian cotton skirt draped just right, her long hair, bangles, and fringes artfully natural. At first, Lisa thought he had followed his British girlfriend there, but he said no. Israel had been his idea. The girlfriend, who hadn't been enthusiastic about working on a kibbutz in the first place, was obviously sick of it. When she noticed Gerhardt and Lisa looking at each other across the table at lunch, she had a carefully orchestrated fit and took off for Tel Aviv to catch a flight home.

Soon after that, Lisa moved in with him. What had she been thinking? Well, of course, she'd fallen for him. He was handsome in a way she'd always admired, tall, with lovely wide shoulders tapering to a slender waist. He had long hair then, a beard trimmed to highlight a stubborn chin, an extraordinary, wicked smile. And he was nice, in spite of a physical laziness, a tendency to lounge. But really, hooking up with a German in Israel?

The fact was, at that age she thought World War II was long past, that thirty years held eons, that so much time had gone by the war was all history. Like many North Americans, she hadn't learned much about any of it in the first place.

The *kibbutzniks* tolerated the foreign volunteers rather irritably, not expecting much but taking any work they came up with for granted. The volunteers were housed in a complex of cement blocks, rooms surprisingly private, and spacious because furnishings were almost non-existent. She started out living in the singles' quarters with an Australian girl, Francine, as a roommate. They got along all right but were so different they didn't become friends. Francine got up at six every morning to fix her hair and do her makeup. She'd broken up with her boyfriend in order to do the long tour so many Australians seemed to feel obliged to undertake, but she talked about him volubly and obsessively. "Why on earth didn't he come with you?" Lisa finally asked.

"He has no money and never will," Francine said. "And so I should get over him. I want to have a big house and nice things, eventually."

Then Francine had bad news from home. Her ex-boyfriend had been in a car accident. He would be in traction for months, and there was likely brain damage. She left immediately for Melbourne.

"Maybe now that he has brain damage they'll have more in common," Lisa said.

Cleaning caked dirt from his gloves, Gerhardt raised his eyebrows before he grinned.

Soon after that, they moved into a new room in the couples' complex, where they found a mattress, two mismatched chairs, an unpainted table, and on a closet shelf a crumpled rag that turned out to be a worn soldier's shirt. Once washed, it fit her perfectly.

She didn't much like helping out in the kitchen, but it was preferable to the alternative, child care. The children were raised as they were educated, in large groups, as if each child belonged to a family of twelve or so but were all of the same age. They assembled in long, chattering queues snaking from one activity to another, and slept together in dorms at night. Who knew when they saw their parents? Early on she'd filled in for someone and soon realized that she didn't have the necessary air of authority to keep those kids in line.

Near the kibbutz was one of the most beautiful beaches in the country, where one afternoon she helped to watch over a group of kite-flying eight-year-olds. A vast golden beach led to waves of molten silver doubling the intensity of the sun, with multicoloured diamond silhouettes against a cloudless sky: the children careening like tops spinning away a few hours of freedom from routine, their noise carried away by the wind. They couldn't understand her and weren't listening anyway. Their housemother yelled herself hoarse, while Lisa, giving up, borrowed a kite to fly. She kept an eye out when any of them went for a swim, and hoped for the best. When they got back, she knew she'd be relegated to the kitchen for good. She didn't mind. She didn't intend to be at the kibbutz long, and kitchen work was busy but mindless. She was responsible mainly for peeling and chopping vegetables in a cavernous mess hall which, in spite of its few windows, seemed too bright, and every sound echoed. The clatter of cutlery and crockery in that building came to embody the word cacophony. On the positive side, this meant it was almost impossible to hold a long conversation.

One day a thin, middle-aged woman Lisa had noticed practising yoga on the lawn and riding her bicycle to the garden tapped her on the shoulder. "You must please ask your boyfriend to keep his voice down," she said. "Even if he is speaking English." She walked away without explanation.

"He's not a loud person," Lisa said to Rivka, the supervisor, who was standing beside her tearing leaves off wilted lettuce. "Is he?"

"Esther is a survivor," Rivka said. "Of Dachau. She finds it difficult to hold on when there are such reminders." She grabbed one of Lisa's thrown-away leaves. "This is perfectly good food," she said, tearing it into the salad.

Lisa gazed off into the main dining hall, where people were beginning to come in hungry for lunch, the volunteers straggling, the *kibbutzniks*, no matter what their ages, noisy and wired to a higher tension. Where did they get all that energy? A healthy diet? Constant exposure to others? Right then she was sick of them all.

"You know that lady who's always meditating by the garden?" she asked Gerhardt that afternoon.

"Yes." He was absently looking for something in a pocket of his backpack, in a bad mood because he'd been late for work weeding potatoes and had been told he would have to spend the next few days in the kitchen.

"She's a survivor of Dachau. She asked me to tell you not to speak so loud."

He found what he was looking for, a scrunched safari hat. "It's time to leave here," he said, and started packing.

"Well, we can't go right now, just like that."

"Why not? We don't have anything of theirs." Vie not. He continued to pack. "Are you coming or staying?"

After that sort of blank ultimatum, why had she gone with him? She couldn't understand it then, or later, and can't now. Was she so much in love by then? She supposed too that she was eager to get away from the kibbutz herself, and his sudden rush to get out of there put her in a panic not to be left. She didn't have time to think. She packed up and followed him, several steps behind, out to the highway. They passed Rivka and a few volunteers on their way to the garden. "We're off," Lisa called the obvious, hurrying after Gerhardt like a caricature of a downtrodden wife.

Remembering brings it all back: the state she was in, her impotent anger. Even then she knew the last straw had as much to do with his being sentenced to several days in the kitchen as with Esther's request.

"Why did you come here anyway?" she yelled at his back.

He stopped for a moment, waited for her, and said he didn't know.

All these years with him. What if she'd just let him go off on his own? She wouldn't have been stranded—she could easily have remained on the kibbutz and worked as long as she wanted. She could have taken up with an American, or another Canadian. Or stayed single. She could have lived a normal life, not had to deal with any Germans but the watered-down variety of her own relatives.

Even though the Israel of the mid-seventies had been allowing German citizens into the country for only a few years, Israelis were surprisingly blasé about having young Germans travelling in their country. After she and Gerhardt started hitchhiking, they met with a hospitality that should have mystified her, but at the time she was so ignorant she took it for granted. Some of the people who picked them up spoke Yiddish, and they chatted away with Gerhardt as if he were a distant, rather unusually interesting cousin.

Both Arabs and Jews seemed to have a strangely jaundiced view of their own country. They would agree with Lisa and Gerhardt about the beauty, the diversity of the Israeli landscape as the young travellers recounted their experiences camping in the desert by Eilat, kayaking on the Red Sea, ascending Mount Masada, floating like human inner tubes in the salty murk of the Dead Sea. But eventually their hosts would say something like, "But the people..." They'd shake their heads sadly. "The people!" At first she thought they were being amiably disingenuous, including themselves in this judgement. But later, she understood they meant everybody other than themselves. They didn't like the recent influx of Moroccan Jews, the Russian immigrants, the Hassidic fundamentalists, the Western liberals. Or, of course, the Palestinians, whose own hostility covered all of the above.

Israelis also resented, in a complicated way because they relied on their donations, the Jewish tourists tanning on the beaches, sightseeing in Jerusalem, touring the settlements and *kibbutzim*, who'd come to the country to assure themselves there was now a homeland but had no intention of moving there. "They come to visit," a truck driver told Gerhardt in Yiddish, "they donate money, and then they go back to New York, happy to be home. They don't fight. They don't work for their country."

"They work for their money," Gerhardt said.

The truck driver nodded but didn't reply.

They reached Jerusalem in spring. The golden Dome of the Rock was visible from almost everywhere, giant cedars graced the outskirts, ancient stone walls surrounded the old city. The Arab medina was still vital, used as a market the way it had been for two thousand years. Donkeys carried dry goods in baskets. Turkish delight lay in purple bricks beside orange and yellow pyramids of spice, slabs of flatbread, fresh mint, vendors calling from neighbouring stalls selling carpets or silver jewellery "I give you student price. Where you from?" Once, when Gerhardt answered "Germany," a man wearing a *djellaba* came over and shook his hand. "You Germans," he said. "You had the right idea."

Gerhardt snorted. With surprise, Lisa hoped. She walked on, stopping at a silver dealer's stall to look at earrings, the merchant offering special prices just for her. When Gerhardt caught up, they left the medina, his face set with a look she couldn't read. His green-blue eyes had chilled, looking grey in the afternoon light. They found refuge in a small park with benches and rose bushes set in decorative gravel, walled in with wrought iron and stone, where they sat silent. None of it had anything to do with him, she thought. Luxurious roses, clouds of yellow, red, pink, seemed weird, alien, the blooms absurdly large for such spindly shrubs.

Touring the city, they watched from above people worshipping at the Wailing Wall. Hassidic men bowed repeatedly, pressing their foreheads against the rough stone and chanting, their long side curls bobbing, fringes of their prayer shawls lifting with the breeze. They too seemed alien, beings from another world altogether. Because of the extreme military presence there, they didn't try to get into the Dome of the Rock. Israeli soldiers armed with automatic weapons swarmed the grounds in larger numbers than the worshippers, and it all seemed too daunting even for a pair of foolish Western tourists.

They stayed in a dank cement youth hostel until the night before they were leaving, when they found a tourist office and decided to splurge on a bed-and-breakfast place. The young woman at the desk looked over at a colleague arranging brochures and they both nodded, obscurely amused. "We have just the place for you," she said. "You're just the type of people Magda Altner is looking for." She made a phone call and then pointed out the route to the apartment, her perfect long red fingernail travelling efficiently over the map.

Magda Altner turned out to be an elderly German Jew, a tiny block of a woman with a hump on her back who was, Lisa soon realized, insane. She welcomed them at the door of her small apartment, exclaiming "Such lovely children! Come in, come in!" But it was Gerhard she adored on sight. She chatted with him in German, using the formal *Sie* for "you" but insisting they call her by her first name. Deciding to include Lisa by speaking very proper English, she began to talk about her upper-class German education, having been raised among the right sort of people. She could see Gerhardt knew how to behave, she said, patting her iron-grey bun. This was news to her, Lisa said, and while Gerhardt grinned, Magda gave her an unreadable stare.

After *Tee und Kuchen*, while Gerhardt was allowed to go immediately to their room and read, the old woman sat Lisa down among her assemblage of knick-knacks and overstuffed furniture and proceeded to describe her girlhood, her father, and the aristocrats they'd known in Germany. "Our apartments were beautiful, with charming wallpaper and hardwood floors gleaming like glass. I had my own room, with a carpet of deep magenta pile. I remember kneeling on it, looking out the window at my sister walking in the garden with that baron of hers. Now what was his name? My memory isn't what it used to be. Baron Hoffstätter. He was smitten with her, absolutely smitten. But Papa would have none of it. She was too young, he said." She looked down for a moment. "Our Papa was strict, but he was a saint. An angel." She changed the subject then, went on about the lack of manners in modern Israeli youth.

Recalling her now, Lisa is struck by the similarities between Magda's memories and those of Gerhardt's grandmother. The same nostalgia for a lost world of gentle refinement, that cultured hothouse environment of the German middle classes. Their heartbroken longing for a past in which they were loved and spoiled by German *Papas*. German fathers, including those who were Jewish, seemed to hold a rather maudlin propensity to cherish their young that seemed inborn. *O mein Papa*. She saw it in Karl with his grandchildren, and she has seen it with Gerhardt. She has never met anyone of the other stereotype, the cold and clinical German, in all the years she's been visiting the country. The Fatherland.

Lisa couldn't imagine what the old woman's real story might have been. How on earth had she escaped the gas chamber, being not only Jewish but handicapped? Had some German aristocrat hidden her? Helped her escape? It wasn't just because Lisa was young and self-centred that she hadn't asked any questions. Magda hadn't allowed a word in edgewise.

After an hour, or maybe two, since Lisa had lost all sense of time, the old woman sat forward, her expression taking on a glazed look that felt copied from her own face. "Have you been saved?" she asked.

"From what?" Lisa absently examined a porcelain figurine of a rosy-cheeked boy fishing. The old woman smiled beatifically and commenced preaching the gospel of Jesus Christ. She seemed to consider her to be prime material for conversion.

Cross-eyed with the effort of trying to appear polite while taking in only a fraction of Magda's sermon, she made one inane comment too many, and the old woman pronounced her stupid and sent her to bed. Released, though with hurt feelings, she found Gerhardt asleep. She woke him, and they made giggly, snorting love, stifling their noise against the scratchy polyester frills of the bedspread.

Breakfast was typical Israeli fare, with yogurt, fruit, hummus, and pita bread. But the coffee was German, thick-looking and black, and Gerhardt had several cups. Magda brought out rolls and marmalade at the end, watching him hungrily as if he were a much loved, rarely seen relative.

A deliveryman came to the door, and Magda communicated with him in English, although he had a hard time understanding her. She didn't speak Hebrew, she told them. She'd moved to Jerusalem twenty years ago, but by then had grown so tired, she couldn't manage yet another language.

As they were leaving, she grabbed Lisa's wrist and said, nodding toward Gerhardt, "Take good care." Lisa has never been sure if she meant "Take good care of him," or if she said, "Take care," as a warning.

SEVEN

She looks through her CDs and puts on Stéphane Grappelli, but tonight finds his vivacious swing annoyingly cheerful. She turns on the TV and watches a show featuring pretend castaways.

The phone rings. An unfamiliar number. "Hello?" she answers, distant and wary.

"Hi, Mom. How are you?"

"Stephanie." She has to catch her breath. It has been what? Six months since her last call? "I'm fine," she says. "How are you? We haven't heard from you in a long time."

"I'm doing great."

The ensuing silence lasts a split second too long, but it's a relief to hear from her, to know she is well enough to sound normal over the phone. "It's good that you called. I've been getting lonely here; your dad's up north on that contract we emailed you about."

"Oh. Well. So, uh, Dad's not there then?"

"No, but I can give you the number of the school he's working in. How are you doing? Still in Nelson?"

"Yes. Kelvin is a snowboarder, like, it's great for him here in winter. We're looking for a better place than this basement suite we're in, but it's hard to find anything near enough to the restaurant I work at."

"So you're doing pretty well then?"

"Yeah. Well, I was, uh, wondering—" She stops abruptly.

Lisa knows she is going to ask for money and almost hangs up. Stephanie knows this. Their conversation would go nowhere, and would upset her for days. "So what is it?"

"I'm registering for college here. Like, I'll be going in the fall."

"What? Really?" Lisa hears her own voice squeak with eagerness.

"Yes, so, uh…I need to access that RESP you saved for me. That education fund?"

"You can't access it until you've gone through the first semester, or whatever, with passing grades."

"I don't remember Tyler having to do that."

"That's the way it is." It's true as far as Lisa is concerned, and Stephanie can't get hold of any of the money without her. "So it's wonderful that you're signing up for a course. You can send me your grades once you've got them."

Silence. Then, "You know I'm doing way better here than I was in Saskatoon."

"I hope so, Stephanie."

"I really am going to take classes in the fall, Mom."

Lisa tries to let hope leave as easily as it slipped in. She would phone the college in June to see if Stephanie's registered. "So. What sort of course is it?"

"It's, uh, it's called a trade discovery program. It's for people who want to see what different skills they might be good at."

This doesn't sound as if it will lead to anything much. "You're not finishing grade twelve?"

"I don't need it for this."

"Well, like I said, once you're in the course you can let me know your marks and then we can see about the RESP. You still owe us for that credit card. Some of it should be used to pay that back."

"Mom. I don't know what you're talking about."

"Stephanie."

"Well, I have to go soon. I'm late for work."

Lisa gives her the Caribou Point phone number and talks about Gerhardt's contract until they hang up. She sits back and turns the TV on mute, blankly following shapes and colours. Nobody but her daughter could produce this hard core of despair, sharpened by anger and regret, and worse yet, tarnished with hope.

When Stephanie was born, Gerhardt took one look at his new daughter and made a sound as if he'd been kicked in the stomach, or dropped from a height. Lisa had seen that look before: when he'd fallen for her in their orange tent in a desert campground in Israel, after they'd already been together over a month. An intensity of tenderness she couldn't—hadn't considered trying to—resist. She saw it happen with Tyler too, a few days after he was born and Gerhardt got up one night to bring him to her. She'd had a hard time with Tyler's birth, and while they were still in the hospital, Gerhardt had been too overwrought with the fallout from her recent pain to focus on the baby. He said, only half joking, that he had post-traumatic stress. But he fell in love with Tyler as intensely as he had with Stephanie. He was a great help with both of them those first years, never questioning his duties as a caregiver, never referring to his having to babysit when she went out, as she'd heard other dads say when they had to look after their own children.

He provided such constant attention to the kids she found it irritating, as if she had three children to consider before she could get anything done. In public, he possessed nothing of the

Canadian way of politely shrugging off or humorously downplaying one's own offspring's complaints. He always made sure the kids came first.

She still can't understand exactly what had happened with Stephanie. She'd been a sensible child, thin and ordinary-looking, bookish, who even as a young adolescent had a teasing, affectionate relationship with both her parents, especially her doting father. Come to think of it, Lisa had expected her to grow up resembling someone like Céline, only wittier. But then, almost suddenly, at age fifteen she transformed. There was nothing obvious, nothing commonplace like removing braces or getting contact lenses. But her features, while remaining essentially the same, modified almost overnight into beauty, her eyes larger and more luminous, her cheekbones higher, her nose newly sculpted. Her figure, though still slender, developed striking curves; even her hair seemed to acquire body, had a new energetic kink to it. At first, Lisa was delighted. But along with Stephanie's new beauty came a new and angry personality, and she began to clash so violently with Lisa and Gerhardt it became routine for her to leave the house altogether. The year she turned sixteen, she stayed at her friend Jennifer's so many days out of each month that Lisa felt they should be giving Jen's mom money for groceries. She should have told Stephanie that the next time she wanted to come home because she couldn't pay her own way, she should be prepared to follow her parents' rules.

But Stephanie's behaviour was Gerhardt's fault too. In fact, he was to blame for taking everything Stephanie said, every snotty teenage utterance, personally. He acted too much like a caricature, a Hollywood German, for Stephanie to resist Nazi references. At first he simply looked shell-shocked, but then his reactions became so sinister they in turn shocked Stephanie, who seemed to assume—and no wonder from her upbringing—that she could get away with anything.

His eyes cold and menacing, Gerhardt would loom over her to give heavy speeches, laying down the law for a change in attitude, for some respect if not obedience. He never had to resort to physical violence because his whole stance threatened it, whether he knew so or not. Lisa spelled this out to him, but he wouldn't hear it. "I have a right to be angry at those things she says. And I can't help what I look like." Lisa reminded Stephanie she was three-quarters German herself, but this had no effect. She read Sylvia Plath and put a star beside the poem "Daddy." She left books on the Holocaust open on the coffee table.

Tyler, of course, locked horns with him too at times, but Tyler was never intimidated and never held grudges. There hadn't been that fraught sulking on both sides that characterized Gerhardt's relationship with Stephanie. He and his son would have a shouting match in the evening, and by the next morning both of them would be working amiably on the car.

Early in their marriage and later during their travels, Lisa had had her own experiences of Gerhardt looming over her, his nonverbal threats, inadvertent or not, provoking such a deep anger she would move closer to him, her face right in his like a baseball player with an umpire, and stare him down. And what had that been but part of his attraction in the first place? That hint of testosterone-washed menace, the possibility of her having to learn to manage him like some young heroine managing the dangerous hero of a romance novel. Heathcliff. At any rate, he had quit looming early on. If anything, over the years she'd become the bully, at least at home, making him toe some sort of line neither of them would be able to articulate. The next time Stephanie called "*Jawohl!*" after Gerhardt told her to drive carefully, Lisa's own hand itched with the urge to slap her.

After about a year, Stephanie's anger seemed to evaporate almost as abruptly as it had started. She developed a casual charm that seemed fraudulent, but Gerhardt was relieved. Always pleasant, she would blithely make promises about drinking or drugs or curfews and then simply go her own way. By the time she was seventeen, she was skipping school and into who knew what drugs. Lisa never knew—she couldn't get a straight answer from Stephanie—whether drugs had fuelled her anger in the first place, or vice versa.

"Hah!" she remembers Stephanie saying once, driven out of her smooth new persona by Lisa's lecturing. "You're always mad at me now because you're not the pretty one anymore."

"That is so ridiculous it doesn't deserve a reply," Lisa told her.

She wonders now if there was an iota of truth there. No. True or not, now with her piercings and tattoos, Stephanie is surely doing her best to give her back that particular status in the family.

After Stephanie gave up confrontation, Gerhardt refused to go along with any of the research Lisa was doing, even addictions counselling. They couldn't make her do anything without the threat of kicking her out, he said, and he wouldn't do that. She was just being a teenager. She would grow up. He had done a wide range of drugs himself, back in the day. Between father and daughter and her own natural tendency toward letting things be and hoping they'd improve, Lisa was powerless. At any rate, if they kicked Stephanie out, she'd move in with Josh, the boyfriend in his twenties, who at the time was likely her main drug supplier.

Stephanie quit school in grade eleven and took what was supposed to be a year off to find what she wanted to do. Until recently, she found she wanted to live in a derelict communal house, hang with her friends and various unknown men, do whatever drugs were available, and work off and on as a waitress in a bar.

It was true, what she said to Suzanne. She is much better off with Stephanie living in another province.

The castaways on TV are competing for immunity from banishment, running across floating balance beams to steal baskets from one another. She switches to the news, but keeps the sound off.

··

GERHARDT COMES HOME for Christmas with the news that his contract is to be extended. The computers are not yet behaving exactly the way they should, not his fault but the manufacturer's. Also, the band council has received extra money for educational purposes and wants more people from the community to take his class.

After his initial pleasure at being home, he sinks into his armchair and binges on TV, even watching afternoon shows like *Judge Judy* and *The Price is Right*. He didn't have a decent television at the school, he says, and when he was able to watch at someone's house, he had to see whatever they were interested in, which was often sports, so that was okay, but still.

Lisa cooks a turkey for Christmas dinner even though it is just the two of them. It's her favourite meal; also roast turkey is one of the easier things to cook, so she isn't about to give up their Christmas treat. Tyler and Céline are still in Europe, travelling in Spain and Morocco, which is a worry, but it's winter and the weather there, Tyler said, is fine. Stephanie can't afford to come home, which Lisa and Gerhardt agree is just as well, but don't look at each other when they say so. Neither of them suggests buying her a ticket.

They are invited to a New Year's party in Saskatoon and are tempted to go. They could spend a couple of days in the Parktown hotel, maybe even splurge on the Bessborough, visit old friends, and celebrate the extension of Gerhardt's contract. But then the Weather Channel forecasts a storm, so they stay home. In the middle of January, he returns to Caribou Point.

..

ONE OF THE WAYS Gerhardt was able to convince Lisa to move out into the country, away from Saskatoon with its city conveniences and old friends, was to find her ideal house. The fact that Suzanne lived in Prince Albert was the deal clincher, but really, as soon as Lisa had a tour of the sprawling bungalow sided with narrow half-logs and surrounded by a neglected garden, she fell in love. She hadn't realized she had a perfect house lodged in her psyche. She'd thought she was content with the old two-storey in which they'd raised the kids.

She liked their old house, had developed an affection for it, was happy simply to be a homeowner. But as soon as she saw this one, she knew she had put up with cramped rooms and creaky floors, outdated plumbing and ugly carpet in the bedrooms because she felt, even though they'd lived there for twenty years, that it was a stopgap.

That was over eight years ago. Now she sits with her coffee listening to stillness, admiring the spacious living room with its white walls and hardwood, the houseplants framing the picture window, the colour-splashed area rugs and soft grey couch and chair she still thinks of as new. The only painting she ever did that she knows for sure is good hangs over the couch. She is a dabbler, has a gift for various creative endeavours, but only to a certain extent. A knack for writing prose that is, well, prosaic; an ear for music but can't read it and has only ever learned three chords on the guitar. Some technical skill in painting, maybe even some talent, but something is missing: Feeling? Perspective? A sense of design?

She thought for years she could become a real painter if she tried but didn't love it enough, couldn't focus.

After she moved to the acreage, she took to gardening and thought maybe that was it, her vocation. Normally she isn't what anyone would call a hard worker, but she happily dug new plots by hand, hauled compost, peat moss, and half-rotted leaves and dug it all into the sandy soil, spread mulch, weeded, fertilized, deadheaded, watered. She always spends January days going though gardening books and planning for the next year. She can lose herself in the garden in a way she has never been able to with anything else.

Her painting on the wall, based on the view from her Aunt Gemma's old bedroom, seems now to be a prediction of her garden. A window with sheer side curtains and a highly polished dark wooden sill looks out on a garden of stylized plants, each one starkly outlined, only on the verge of blooming except for three spectacular orange lilies. She examines the painting with the pride of a creator, thinking how well it fits into this room, how it isn't everybody who is able to craft even one satisfactory object in their lives.

She listens to the stillness, knows she should enjoy this absolute solitude, but lack of anticipation enhances the silence. Nobody, no one but herself, will come through the door without knocking, not for several months.

She starts reading well into the night, often until two or three in the morning. Some nights she can't sleep at all but lies staring into the dark, worrying. All the things she could have, should have done differently with Stephanie when she was younger. Wondering what her new boyfriend is like, what drugs she is taking, if she is at least eating decently. She hopes Tyler and Céline are smart enough not to smoke any weed in Morocco. Smarter than she was in Spain.

She recalls sitting in a van in an Estepona campground with Maureen and a guy she'd spent a couple of nights with, smoking a joint and being startled by a tap on the window. It was a *Guardia Civil*. He shook his head, mimed taking a toke, and waved his finger at them. They recognized the young cop they'd had a friendly conversation with that morning. He walked away. They made a show of getting rid of their stash in the nearest garbage can. God. She could have spent half her life in Franco's prison system.

When she does doze off, she is awakened by night sweats. She feels devoid of agency, as if someone is playing a video game with her as the protagonist. Except she isn't having any adventures. After a couple of teaching jobs during which she nodded off sporadically behind her desk like a teen on drugs, she phoned the school board and said she wasn't well. She would take a job now and then, but only if she had at least a full day's notice. Now jobs are few and far between.

··

SPRING IS STILL a mild suggestion in the frozen March air when, intending to go for a walk on a sunny day, Lisa is startled on her doorstep by a dog barking. There, bounding down the driveway after a squirrel, is Sport, the neighbours' mongrel, with Marjorie Danielson following. She is taking the dog out for some exercise, she calls, and thought she'd swing by, see how Lisa is doing. Because they live so close to each other, the two women have continued over the years to make sporadic if increasingly unenthusiastic efforts to be friendly. Marjorie radiates a winsome artlessness, a sweet charm that gets on Lisa's nerves, partly because she knows it all could be undermined by a mean comment when she least expects it. On her part, she tends to insult Marjorie inadvertently, out of simple awkwardness, she tells herself. The last time she visited her neighbour, soon after Gerhardt flew back to work, she found Marjorie modelling the dress she'd bought for her oldest son's wedding. Confronted with all that pinkish lace and polyester, Lisa knew full well her face showed nothing but amazement, and then she couldn't come up with anything more effusive to say than that it went really well with her shoes.

Marjorie doesn't forget affronts and in fact seems to relish them. A few years ago, for some reason she gained a ton of weight. Looking like a pallid manatee, she took to complimenting Lisa on her appearance every time she ran into her, just, Lisa believes, to see her uncomfortable look as she tried to come up with a compliment for Marjorie. She lost the weight almost as suddenly as she'd gained it, and is now her buxom self, a redhead with a Scottish lassie look that is standing her well into middle age. With her freckled cheeks flushed with exercise, she looks wholesome today, youngish.

"You're sure looking good," Lisa says, for once coming up with something honestly nice, but inadvertently encouraging Marjorie to give her the once-over. She can see Marjorie isn't too impressed and tries to remember when she last washed her hair.

"Thanks!" Marjorie says, now scrutinizing her with satisfied solicitude "So how are *you* anyway?"

"I'm just fine!" She tries not to sound falsely enthusiastic. She bends to pet Sport's sleek head and winces. "Pew."

"He's still pongy from his run-in with a skunk a week ago."

"Ugh. Well, come in for a cup of coffee. I was just going to make a new pot."

Marjorie hesitates and peers down the driveway. "You're likely pretty busy, eh?" Standing there with one hand shading her eyes, she looks like an explorer in a grade-six history book.

"I was just going back in the house anyway," Lisa says. "Sport can amuse himself out here for a bit." She is somewhat taken aback at her own insistence, but realizes it's either have coffee or go for her walk, but with Marjorie.

As she makes herself busy in the kitchen, she searches for something innocuous to talk about. There is, of course, the son's wedding, but she's not sure she wants to remind Marjorie of the dress, and anyway it's over a year away. When they last ran into each other in town, Marjorie said they were planning a family reunion this summer.

"So how are the reunion plans going?"

"Huh. It's supposed to be the August 11 weekend, but no one's replied yet. It's Robbie's family, so they think they can just show up at the last minute, or not. But we're planning to have one of those pitchfork fondues, so we really have to know the number of people coming."

"Pitchfork fondue?"

"Yes. This outfit from P.A., they come and heat up a big vat of oil and you can dip your steak in it for as long as you want. I mean, the cook will do it for you. It might be dangerous to have someone like Robbie's brother after a few drinks playing around with a pitchfork, let alone hot oil."

"Oh my god, what a concept."

Marjorie frowns. "Lots of people around here have them, you know. Well, I guess you wouldn't know." After a measured silence, she goes on. "Anyway, the steaks taste great, and they supply all the trimmings, salads and side dishes and that. They'll do chicken and pork chops too, in case there's somebody who doesn't eat red meat."

"I'm sure it's a fantastic idea," Lisa says, trying harder. "Especially when they supply everything."

"So are you planning a trip this summer? Back to Germany maybe?"

"God no. We were just there last fall. More than one visit a year would kill me."

Marjorie smiles on cue, sips her coffee. "So you never really said how your trip went."

"Oh, it was fine. Gerhardt's parents are nice enough. A month is just...well, it's about three weeks too long."

"Yes, I suppose, staying with in-laws the whole time. With Robbie's parents we have to visit way more often, but at least we can escape after an hour or two. I can't imagine having to live with them for a month. On the other hand, you get a trip to Europe out of it with a free place to stay."

"I suppose so, yes."

"I don't imagine Germany as being that popular a destination though. People might still find it hard to get past the history, the Nazis and that." She gives Lisa a quick glance, then looks down. "But of course that was all such a long time ago."

"Yes." She glances at Marjorie's cup to see how much coffee is left, gauging the time until she leaves. She thinks of Gerhardt's grandmother, and Magda from Jerusalem. During the war, they'd have been about the age she and Marjorie are now. She feels a touch of pressure on the back of her neck.

As Marjorie is putting on her jacket, they hear the dog bark, likely at some other animal of interest. "I guess old Sport's stunk up your yard long enough now. I'd better hurry up before he gets into a porcupine." Stepping into her boots, she says, "Give me a call sometime. You know I'm usually at home too." They both know this is just something to say.

..

AFTER ANOTHER ONE of her restless nights, she wakes from soundless depths to a pulsing noise that seems an extension of her unconscious. She fumbles for the phone, checking the call display. It's Gerhardt.

"Lisa? Are you still in bed?"

"No. Uh, yes. I'm not feeling well."

"Headache?"

"Yes."

"Well, I won't keep you long."

She forces some enthusiasm into her voice. "No, no, it's gone now. How's it going? Are you still living in the school?"

"Yes, I don't have much choice." He goes on for a couple of minutes about his living conditions. Then he says, "I had a bit of a... an incident the other night." He hesitates in his teasing way, long enough to make her irritably curious.

"An incident?" Now what? At least he sounds amused, although with Gerhardt that could still mean disaster.

"Yeah, living in a building like this can be a bit weird."

"Weird, how?" From his tone, she bets he is the one who did something weird.

He laughs to himself. "I caught a guy breaking into the school the other night."

"What?"

"I was asleep, but a noise woke me up. Somebody was tampering with the door to the gym. When I got there, I stood in the dark and listened for a minute. Then I didn't want him to wreck the lock, so I shoved the door open and caught him by surprise. I grabbed him in a chokehold and twisted his arm."

"You what!?"

He laughs again. "He just about shit his pants. I said, 'I know who you are. You ever try this again you'll wish you were dead.' He ran off like hell."

"Gerhardt! Are you nuts?"

"He was just a high school kid I think, seventeen or eighteen. I have no idea who he was, really."

"For God's sake, there could have been a whole gang of them!"

"Well, there wasn't. I would have heard them shuffling around or talking while picking the lock." He makes another of his hesitations. There is more to come. "But then I found myself in some real trouble."

"What?" she asks, her tone now the amused disdain he is looking for.

"We were outside on the steps. When he ran off, the door slammed shut behind me. Locked, of course. It was three in the morning and twenty-five below. There I was, in my sock feet, a T-shirt, and pair of sweat pants."

"Oh for Christ's sake!"

"But the school's right near some houses, so I just walked into the nearest one, Dadzene's. I called out that I'd locked myself out. Cyrus Dadzene woke up and said go sleep on the couch, there's a blanket on it already. So that's what I did. It was a big joke the next day."

"Why on earth didn't you just pound on the door and make him run off while you were still inside?"

"I was too pissed off," he says. "Acted on instinct."

EIGHT

Gerhardt won't be home until the end of June; he is now teaching computer classes for school kids and acting as an advisor to any teachers who still need help. She hasn't yet worked up the energy to clear the garden, although the weather turned beautiful in April and has stayed that way. Out contemplating the work that needs to be done, feeling tired just thinking about all the cutting and raking, she is interrupted by Sport, barking with his usual enthusiasm in the middle of the driveway. Marjorie again, she thinks, even though it has been almost two months since her last visit. As they exchange pleasantries, Lisa is on the verge of inviting her in, but Marjorie puts up her hand, as if to stall her.

"I'm just stopping by for a minute, really. I wanted to ask a favour."

"Oh? Well, sure." Within reason. Are she and Robbie going somewhere and need her to feed the dog? At least that would give her an incentive to go for a walk every day. But they'd have to get their other neighbour for the cattle anyway so...

"I'm going away on Tuesday, to Calgary to visit Janine, but I forgot I was booked to work at Pioneer Village for a couple of days. I volunteer with them, you know, to help out?"

"Oh?" Janine is Marjorie's sister. Lisa can see where this is going and isn't sure what to say.

"I give old people rides to appointments and help in the kitchen and with the yardwork and that. Visit with a couple of them. I'm supposed to help dig the gardens and do some planting next week, but I forgot all about it when I was making plans for Calgary."

"Oh. Well, gardening." At least she could see herself doing that. What the hell, she could use some distraction. "Yes, I could fill in for you if you want. I wouldn't mind driving people around either if they need that," she adds, feeling generous.

"Oh thanks, Lisa! I was really in a bind there. I wouldn't want to piss off Alice."

"Alice Jointon?"

"Yes. She heads up the volunteer program there. I have her office phone number written somewhere." She digs in her jacket pocket and hands Lisa a slip of paper.

"I'll get the times and details from her then."

"Yeah, it's just for three days or so, then I'll be back the week after. Thanks so much for this, Lisa. Nobody else had any time." After a slightly awkward pause, Lisa invites her in for coffee. For once she has the advantage, has a small sense of the pious self-satisfaction that Marjorie must live with all the time.

"No more coffee for me, I've had too much already. I'm kind of in a rush, have to go to town in an hour. But is it okay if I just use your bathroom?"

"Sure." Lisa's smugness deflates as she tries to recall the last time she cleaned the sink and toilet. People should always call before coming over.

••

LISA KNOWS Alice Jointon as a solid, motherly looking sort of woman, one of those officious browbeaters who could steamroll right over her, leaving her flatly performing work that nobody else wanted. She would have to be blunt, upfront, and stubborn-sounding about doing only gardening or she'd end up wiping drool off chins at meal times. "Would you be willing to do some work in the kitchen?" Alice's voice has a hopeful, almost greedy note to it. Apparently, there is a dearth of people willing to help out for free. Alice is hoping she might be able to add her to the permanent roster.

Thinking of her days on the kibbutz, she figures she could handle being a kitchen aide, but only under dire circumstances. "No, I'm afraid not," she answers pleasantly. She has on her most businesslike telephone voice. "I'd be no good at any, uh, caregiving in the nursing home, either. I'm willing to drive people to appointments and errands with a day or more's notice, and I'd be happy to help out with the gardening. Marjorie said that's what I'd be filling in for her for."

After a short silence, Alice says yes, well then she should come on Tuesday to help put in the garden. "Be here at nine sharp," she says tersely.

Take it or leave it, Lisa prevents herself from commenting. "All right. I can park right in front of the nursing home in visitors' parking?"

Alice agrees. "You might as well go straight to Ben Meisner's place—he does the gardening here. He's at number nineteen, one of the duplexes on the south side. I'll tell him you'll be coming."

..

LIKE ALL THE OTHER doors in the seniors' complex, Ben Meisner's has been painted a shiny, violet-hued blue, the trim the same colour. He greets her with, "So. You are Mrs. Braun." He is a heavy man, balding, fallen with age toward his centre. He wears dark-rimmed glasses that slightly magnify his eyes, and his face has traces of a farmer's tan.

"Yes. Lisa." She shakes his hand. "Mr. Meisner. How do you do." She is spurred into formality by his manner and a slight accent. German? A hint of Europe, anyway, and he didn't tell her to call him Ben.

"We have a very nice day for gardening," he says, waving at the outdoors as if he has conjured it up for her benefit, and she agrees.

He grabs a Co-op cap, steps out of slippers, and lowers himself onto an old piano stool in the entranceway to put on a pair of well-worn hiking boots. "Don't worry, we're not going on a long trek. I need these boots for support even if I only walk to the post office."

He walks faster than she expected, and within a minute or two they reach the annual flower garden, a large, square area fronting the main building, with ornate wrought iron–and–wood benches and gravel paths. "I always plant this plot early," he says, "but I cover them if it freezes, and plants such as snapdragons are cold-hardy anyway."

"I always thought they hired a professional to do all this."

"That would be me," he says, bending slowly to pull a sow this-tle. "They hire me, at a very small price I must say, to design and plant their gardens. After we sold the farm, I used to supplement my income doing odd jobs for a garden centre in Prince Albert, but now I work only here. Come. I will show you the perennial and vegetable plots behind the nursing home. Just leave your spade and fork here—we'll be returning to do this one first."

··

ONCE HE SEES she knows what she is doing, he leaves her to dig a plot on her own. She's happy not to have to make conversation. She turns over the black loam, which had been covered with compost in the fall, then stops to watch Mr. Meisner working on the other end of the garden. Contemplating the number of plots needing to be done, she regrets for a moment that she isn't turning over the less impressive loam of her own garden. But she puts her head down and works, getting into the rhythm, and eventually meets Ben Meisner in the centre. "I guess we're supposed to go for lunch in the cafeteria or whatever?" she asks. She's quite hungry but isn't looking forward to the conversation she'd be forced to make with people who might or might not be familiar. Not to mention having to report on their progress to Alice Jointon.

"Ach, no," he says. "We'll have lunch at my place. Even when the food is decent, I don't like communal eating. All that chit-chat."

"Good." She grins at him. "I'd much rather we eat by ourselves too."

It is sunny but still cool. The lawn is turning green; the lilac and caragana shrubs surrounding the nursing home and front garden are beginning to leaf out. The perennials Mr. Meisner has planted in his own small front garden plot are pushing through the mulch.

They have canned tomato soup and grilled cheese sandwiches, continuing their independent partnership with Mr. Meisner allowing her to heat up the soup. Through an open doorway she can see the clean lines of his checkered couch and La-Z-Boy. His TV is set on a homemade stand of blond oak that matches the kitchen table. As he is setting the table, he moves a book onto the counter, one that she has recently read. "Oh! You're reading Richard Ford."

He nods and puts the sandwiches down, concentrating, and Lisa realizes how tired he is. He has been keeping up with her, she thinks, and might have overdone it. "Yes," he says. "I enjoy his sense of humour."

They sit down to eat and continue to chat about books, then trade plant lore and discuss the merits of compost and leaf mould for their sandy soil and the best depth to transplant irises. They rest a while before getting back to work. When they return to the garden, she's concerned about him becoming overtired. She tries not to let him see her watching him, and his air of stubborn purpose prevents her from commenting. Really, it is none of her business; he is a grown-up. But before two o'clock, she calls to him, "I'm just about ready to pack it in. We don't have to do all this in a couple of days, you know. I can keep coming back for shorter times until it's done."

He nods and starts cleaning the soil off his spade, not bothering to object. "Good. That's good. I'm no spring chicken, as they say."

She thinks of offering to work for a day by herself but doesn't. "Neither am I. I'll feel all this by tomorrow morning." She stows her tools in the trunk of her car, then returns to the garden, where Mr. Meisner is now sitting on a bench. "Why don't we just work half days?" she asks. "Morning or afternoon, doesn't matter to me."

He now looks pale and exhausted, and she regrets not suggesting this at lunch. "Afternoons might be best," he says. "Then we can sleep in and have all the coffee we need. Besides, we can also then have a drink together after work."

"Yes!" She is unexpectedly pleased at the thought.

••

DRIVING HOME, she recalls with some pleasure the spongy dark loam she has spent the day turning over. The compost came from a couple of giant bins behind the nursing home. She knows the health of the soil is Mr. Meisner's doing, that he's been taking care of it for years. She didn't ask him how long he's been in Canada or where he is from. Gerhardt is always being asked where he's from, and it gets on his nerves. He usually says, "Saskatoon."

She's pretty sure, with his slight accent and the name Meisner, that he is German.

She enjoyed being with him, and is glad, for once, that Marjorie asked her for a favour. She looks forward to tomorrow.

··

THE NEXT AFTERNOON, they finish digging the annual garden. Tomorrow they'll do the vegetable garden, and add old manure, already waiting in a pile by the compost bins, to the perennials. When she suggested dividing the work into half days, it hadn't occurred to her that Marjorie would be back before they finished. She and Mr. Meisner work closer together today, companionable but still mostly silent. "Marjorie Danielson will be back on Tuesday," she says, "but I'd like to finish all this with you, planting out the seedlings and everything."

"Yes, of course. I'd much rather..." He stops. "Now that you've started you might as well finish, eh?"

She grins at him. "Maybe you can tell that to Alice."

"Oh. Alice."

"I'll mention it to her as well. She'll think she's snared another permanent volunteer."

They stop at four. "It's time for a drink," he suggests. "I have beer and wine in the fridge."

"Oh good!" They clean their tools and wander slowly toward the duplex. "So you've worked with Marjorie before?" she asks.

"Oh yes."

"She probably told you we're neighbours?"

"Yes." He smiles rather enigmatically. "I know all about you and your German husband. You have a son and a daughter."

No doubt Marjorie gossiped about Stephanie. "And you?" she asks. "You have something of a German accent, I think?"

"I am originally from Minden, south of Bremen. Do you know the area?"

"Not really; Gerhardt is from Berlin. You'll have to meet him when he gets back from his contract up north." He looks hesitant and she thinks she is being forward. A bit too open to socializing.

He nods. "Did Marjorie tell you I'm a Jew?"

"Well, no." She can't think of anything to say. "She didn't say a thing about you, didn't even mention who the gardener was that I'd be working for."

"With," he says. "You've been working with me, not for. And doing very well, I must say." He raises his glass.

"Thank you." She raises her wine glass too. He is being generous. His praise has dispersed the awkwardness that usually surfaces when she or Gerhardt meet someone Jewish, and she is thankful for it. She wonders if he escaped Germany before the war or emigrated after, and decides it would be okay to ask. "So you moved here after the war?"

"Yes. After I met my wife, who was from here." He waves as if scattering a cloud of mosquitoes. "But that was a long time ago. Now I want only to stay put. And to plant gardens." He gets up from his chair with some difficulty and retrieves a folder from his coffee table. "I have here the landscape plan for the annuals."

She examines the diagram and makes a few suggestions, but he says, "Too much symmetry isn't good. You will see once it's all flowering how much more beautiful is a little chaos."

••

"RICHARD FORD is all very well, but there is another American I have discovered. Have you read William Gass?"

"No. Or maybe I might have read an essay or two of his when I was taking classes."

"I will lend you *The Tunnel*. It's his magnum opus. Very long."
He takes it from his bookshelf. "One long rant. Terrible main character, but formed from the same clay as Gass himself. A brave book. It took him thirty years to write."

She weighs it in her hands. "Hmm. A doorstop. It will have to grab me—I might have to take my time."

"You'll have all the time you need."

"'Opa's Magnum,'" she says. "I always thought that would make a good title for a story about a German grandfather who'd confiscated an American's magnum gun during the war."

He smiles and shakes his head. "A terrible pun. But you should write it."

"No. I'm a reader, not a writer."

"Have you tried?"

"Oh yes. Everything I write sounds banal. There's a certain poetic spark I just don't have. I've tried painting as well. Got some talent for depiction, but not, uh…Maybe I'm just not dedicated enough to overcome my shortcomings."

"But you could if you tried."

"I'm afraid not." She smiles ruefully. "No, literally: I'm afraid. But enough of my neuroses. Let's look at the seeds we need for the vegetables."

While they work, he becomes more loquacious, talking about the hardiest plants for their area, the best way to improve soil, how to take care of tools. Lecturing a little; Germans are champion explainers, she thinks, but then feels uncharitable. He's had training and a lifetime of experience. "You see my spade compared to yours? How sharp it is? We must sharpen yours at the next break. Sharp tools are as necessary for the garden as for the kitchen." She doesn't tell him she hates sharp kitchen knives. She always uses a serrated steak knife to cut vegetables or she'd end up lacking a finger.

But by the end of the day, she feels nothing but gratitude. Deciding to be an enthusiastic student, she has not only learned more about gardening but has had much of her own knowledge validated. "This was like taking a class in horticulture," she tells him at the end of the day. "I should be taking notes."

They would seed the vegetables on her last day. In the meantime, they need a truck or a van to drive to the garden centre to pick up flats of seedlings for the flower beds. They catch Alice as she's coming out of the nursing home at the end of the day. "We used to have the van," Alice says, nodding at Mr. Meisner, "the one we used other years, but it quit on us and we had to get rid of it." She turns to Lisa. "A replacement is not a high priority in our budget."

Without thinking, Lisa says, "Gerhardt's left his work van at home. We can use it. That is," she qualifies, a bit relieved to have an excuse if he said no, "if I can get it started."

••

"I JUST HOPE," she says, wrestling with the steering on the way out of town, "that I don't have to parallel park this thing." They start out in the morning this time, not sure how long everything will take.

"You'll be able to pull into the parking lot," Mr. Meisner says. "They have big flats with wheels, easy to push right up to your vehicle."

"Yes, of course." She has been there herself, plenty of times. They drive in companionable silence. He doesn't seem to be much of a morning person either. She thinks of putting on the radio but can think of nothing she wants to listen to. She glances over and sees him nod off and wake up with a start. He glances at her and grins as if to say, I'm old—what do you expect? He's wide awake with expectation, though, before they reach the garden centre. He has made sure the plants he wants are ready and waiting, and in fact a young man in a denim jacket is there to pack it all in the van. "Hey," he says, smiling at Lisa. "Mrs. Braun."

"Yes?" She looks closely at him, recognizes an old student, and hazards a guess. "Jason?"

"Yep, it's me. How're you doing?" He doesn't wait for an answer but starts shifting flats of petunias.

"Summer job, eh?" She makes a few lacklustre moves to help, but seeing she is just in the way, stands to one side.

"Yep." Jason picks up another flat. "If summer starts in April."

"School in the fall? Tech or university?"

"Nope." He grins. "Just hanging in P.A."

Mr. Meisner is keeping an eye out. "The geraniums can go on top there, so there's more room," he suggests.

"Okay." Jason crawls amiably into the van to rearrange.

The cashier knows Mr. Meisner. "So they've still got you slaving away up there, eh Ben? Too young and spry to pack it in?" She winks at him as she hands him the bill.

He smiles slightly and signs. "We're all set," he says to Lisa.

"Okay, let's get this show on the road," she says, feeling as if some of the cashier's fatuous good humour has worn off on her. Driving down Central Avenue, she says, "I was going to suggest going somewhere for lunch, but I guess these seedlings should be set in the shade as soon as possible." A car honks at her as she changes lanes.

"Also, it's likely best you drive this vehicle straight out of town."

"Ha ha." Teasing or not, though, he is right. She's relieved when they are finally parked at the side of the nursing home. It takes them an hour to unpack and make sure every little pot is watered. "Let's go for lunch in the cafeteria today," he says.

"Yes. It's late—there won't be many people left eating."

Walking into the dining hall, the first person they see is Marjorie. "Well hello, Ben!" She is stacking her tray and waves at them across the room. At least she's done eating. "Hi, Lisa." She eyes Lisa for a split second and turns to Mr. Meisner with a proprietary air. "So, you've had her working pretty hard, eh?"

"Oh yes." Mr. Meisner smiles benignly on both women. "She knows as much about gardening as I do, but it pleases her to say she's my student."

"Huh, that's not just something to say," Lisa says. "I've learned so much in the last few days, I feel as if I've been taking a course. We're going to plant all the seedlings this afternoon and tomorrow, then clean up and work the perennial garden and do the vegetables. On Thursday we should be done." She considers saying she hopes that's okay with Marjorie, but then realizes the best approach is simply to assume. "We should have been finished by now but decided to work only a few hours a day." She knows that Marjorie is on the verge of offering to help so, beginning to sidle toward the kitchen, she says abruptly, "We'd better grab some food before they close right down." She makes sure Mr. Meisner is in front of her. As they make their escape, she turns and calls, "Come over for coffee sometime, Marjorie," without really looking at her.

"Sorry," she says, cutting into her cutlet. "That was a bit awkward, but Marjorie was going to offer to help us finish. I just couldn't face a whole couple of days working with her."

"I'm happy," he says. "Mrs. Danielson is a perfectly nice woman, but I'd rather work only with you."

She knows he is being gracious but decides to believe him.

••

THEY PLANT SEEDLINGS all afternoon and run overtime to five o'clock. "Maybe we should have asked Marjorie to help," she says over her wine at the end of the day. She lifts her glass. "Tomorrow I'm bringing the wine."

"No, I have a nice supply, and I am very glad to share it." He pours her a second glass. "I developed a taste for wine from my mother. She had a French cousin she visited as a teenager every summer. French wine and cuisine. She was a very good cook, my mother." A shadow crosses his face, and Lisa wonders again about his family during the Holocaust. "She could have been a professional," he continues.

"What did your father do?"

"He was a landscaper and gardener." He examines his glass and puts it down without drinking. "I learned from him. Until the war of course. Then everything fell apart."

"Yes." She wants to ask what happened but can't say anything.

"I am a survivor. Of Buchenwald."

"Oh." She says it almost as a response to a blow. *Der Buchenwald.*

He watches her, searching, it seems, for the right reaction. She is pretty sure that the "oh" wasn't it.

He says, "Not too many people know that. Or they know it, but nobody wants to hear about it."

"I would," she says. She realizes that this is true only now. To try to comprehend, to listen to someone sitting right across a table, listen to someone she knows and likes. After all the years with Gerhardt, knowing his family. "I have...I am half German myself, besides being married to one." She tries to explain how it is, how her visits to Europe are always disturbed. "The forest near my in-laws' house, for example—it's a beech forest. Every trip to Germany is shadowed by the Holocaust, whether I'm consciously thinking about it or not. It seeps into everything; it's like a faint odour no one talks about."

"Yes," he nods. "And by the next generation it will dissipate altogether." He takes off his glasses and rubs his eyes. "I will tell you about Buchenwald. But not while we're working. I'll see you tomorrow and Thursday to garden, and you can come for a visit next week. I must have a bit of time to prepare myself. Then I will talk to you about my life in the camp."

Disoriented at this turn of events, she shakes hands with him before she leaves, as if sealing a deal. But now she isn't sure if she is ready to listen to a real person, to have an actual survivor talk to her, talk right in front of her about his experiences.

She walks into her house not recalling anything of the drive home except the sense of doom that accompanied her. What will happen? What more does she really want to learn? She certainly won't be any happier for it. And what will he want in return for his story? There would be something to pay, no matter how intangible. She has no illusions of being psychic, but she has found over the years that no matter how long it takes, a sense of doom always proves to be justified.

NINE

She knocks on his blue door, thinking maybe she should have brought a notebook. But no. This isn't an interview or a research project. She just wants to hear what he has to say, and live with it. He's sitting at his kitchen table and doesn't get up but calls to her to come in. He looks the same as usual. She doesn't know what she expected: that he'd have lost some sleep, as she had? That he'd look haggard?

He doesn't waste any time with preliminaries but tells her he'll say what he has to say, and then that will be it. She understands this isn't to be a conversation, but that's what she expected.

"I am a bitter man, with good reason, but sometimes I believe I was born to bitterness, like an herb whose fate was sealed once it sprouted in dry shade. I look at beauty, face joy, and feel nothing at my core but despair. I have lived like this most of my life now, and I am tired of it.

"What I just said? Ach, it's a lie. I read too much, I get carried away. The fact is, my childhood and early youth were happy enough, and since Buchenwald I've encountered hope, felt kinds of happiness. I married the wife I wanted, had children. I've forced myself to forget and have locked the camp and its horrors away in a corner of my mind for years at a time.

"Now again I remember. Not because you have asked for my story, but because I am old and have few distractions. I could have more to do with others, but I prefer to cultivate a reputation for solitude. To continue to cultivate one: I have been an outsider all my life, even when young. Not because I am a Jew—there were other Jews at school, and also I could have had Gentile friends—but because I have always felt separate from others. A shyness, perhaps, that led to a certain misanthropy, to a preference for being alone. I believe that is why I survived Buchenwald. Once there, I worried about no one but myself.

"These chroniclers, like that Frankl and his search for meaning, they chose what memories to write about. Primo Levi, you've read him? Levi skirted the edge of the chasm when he was young, describing the revulsion of a man he confessed to over a night of talk, but you notice he would not go into details for his readers. What did he confess? What weaknesses, what crimes forced his listener to recoil in such contempt at the end of that long night? Or maybe it wasn't contempt. Maybe in the end his listener hated him for his stark portrait of reality, for pointing out the realities of which man is capable.

"This is part of the legacy the Nazis left me: the shame of knowing the essence of my own evil. Brutalization pared my humanity to its skeleton just as starvation did to my body. I have spoken of none of it to my wife, or to my children. You have appeared in my life right now, and I don't know if it is good or bad, but I am talking in spite of myself, to spite myself, now that I face a so-called peaceful death from old age. I feel no obligation to add to the record, to make sure the world won't forget. The world has already forgotten—or if not, it doesn't care, but goes ahead with its brutalities as always. 'Ethnic cleansing' is a modern term. I am talking to you because right at this time I want to see your face, to see by your face that you acknowledge this happened. To me.

"I was tortured. Flogged for stealing a morsel, bludgeoned on the way to work stations at a quarry, forced to stand perfectly in line, once for eighteen hours straight. How does one describe such things? I can give you the bare facts, and they mean just what they say.

"However. The first time I was beaten, I will tell you. I was gently raised. Yes, gently raised, and along with the shock of seeing children and the elderly receiving the same treatment, all on our way to the cattle cars, this, this first brutality against me was a revelation.

"It was before the beginning of the war. Yes, after *Kristallnacht*, but still, no one, not even Jews, had any idea what would come. What a shock it was. Shock? A catastrophic earthquake. In spite of the prospect of ghettos, the restrictions to which we were already subjected, the prejudices and propaganda, I'd grown up considering myself a German. That wasn't easy to let go of, that identity: a citizen of Germany, and only somewhere down on the list of who I was, Jewish.

"I've told you my father was a gardener—he designed and created landscapes for small businesses, private properties. A gardener was an unusual thing for a Jew to be. In one dialect of Yiddish, there are no words even to differentiate flower species. But my parents didn't speak Yiddish, we spoke High German. I suppose growing up helping my father prepared me for the idea of moving here to Saskatchewan, taking over my in-laws' farm. I thought I knew something about agriculture.

"Yes, I speak English well, and have lost most of my accent. Some people have the facility to lose it, or the desire, and I had both, I suppose. It is hard work to lose a German accent, making the 'th' come naturally. But now, close to the end of my life, I would like to speak my native tongue to someone who could easily reply. It is to your husband I would rather speak. But of course, he would refuse. His generation might acknowledge their parents' guilt but have grown tired of shouldering it.

"But now. The first experience of being beaten. I grew up a sturdy child, not easily cowed on the playground. I went my own way, but earned enough respect to be left alone. I never had to fight.

"I was nineteen years old, a student of philosophy. Or had been until I was not allowed. The soldiers of the SS formed a sort of gauntlet on the way to the train station. Whipped and clubbed, I was blinded with pain, crippled with it. The sick crunch, the thud of cudgel against bone, and somehow after a time, standing outside myself, knowing that's my head, my elbow or shin, and the rage—I would have fought back, but a man near me lashed out at one of his tormentors and was shot dead. Period. You hear the cliché about one's blood running cold, but that's what I remember, my rage chilled by my blood, by terror. I didn't realize then that to be shot stone dead would have been a stroke of luck. I seemed to black out, and once aware again, I found myself in the queue for the cattle car.

"Three days to reach Buchenwald. I had a flask I'd filled with water—I don't recall why I had the sense to do that. It was an old whisky flask of my father's. It may have saved my life—no one else had anything, or if they did it was soon seen and shared.

"Yes, I do recall now why I had the flask. I thought that if the Nazis who forced us to gather in the square wanted to confiscate it, at least they'd be disappointed to find only water. But no one cared about our possessions on the way there. It was later, after we were off the train, that everything we had was stolen.

"Those three days, the heat and the smell, nowhere to relieve ourselves, packed in so we were not able to lie down, barely able to sit, I managed to move next to the outer wall. Yes, I was young and strong, I forced my way next to a seam in the boxcar, and turning toward it, I could breathe a trickle of fresh air, and in the blackest part of those nights, I was able to take lukewarm sips.

"When the doors opened, we poured out. We were treated like sewage—none of the guards meeting us would equate us with human beings. We were dealt with as if we were sewage, treated worse than they would have treated cattle. Elie Wiesel—you've read *Night*? He says that he got used to blows and clubbing, that the pain was deadened after so much, but I don't know. He was once flogged twenty-five times and said after the first few he didn't feel much. He didn't talk about after. Recalling my whippings, I remember nothing but pain. It was pain that one had to learn to live with. Always there. But nothing compared to the hunger.

"I will describe not much more in great detail. Reliving my tortures would cause them to expand like a wetted sponge to take up all the room in myself.

"That train ride in Hell ended up at Buchenwald. You know what the inscription was over the entrance? "To each what is due to him." One thing Frankl got right—you've read his book? In the camps, whenever someone was having a nightmare, if he wasn't bothering us too much, we didn't wake him, because nothing could be more terrible than reality. Yes, you would know, you have read about it, seen documentaries. My head shaved; threadbare, striped clothing; footwear that didn't fit, clogs, too small wooden clogs I had to work in. What can I tell you that you don't already know? Beaten every day on the way to the worksites. Watery grey soup, heels of dry bread, and one had to scrap and negotiate for each morsel.

"The hunger was with us day and night, something alive inside us. We would do anything for an extra piece of gristle, a crust of bread: negotiate, trade, bribe, thieve. Anyone who had no talent or stomach for that sort of thing starved to death early on.

"That was everyday life. The Bunker, the punishment cell-block, I don't know how to describe. To be sent there was a death sentence. An area sectioned off from the rest, where were carried out tortures no one could fathom. I was a Jew caught with extra food, so there I was thrown. I saw fellow Jews buried alive, then killed with shovels when they forced through the earth to breathe. I saw Jews beaten with truncheons into lavatory ditches filled with filth and drowned. Men picked one at a time at random for sport, tortured, made to perform tricks, then forced to run into the forbidden zone to be shot. The guards had quotas. So many must be dead at the end of the day. There were those who ran into the zone intentionally, but that could end in worse agony. One could be shot in the stomach and left for some time before being killed.

"It was there in the Bunker that we were made to stand eighteen hours in the cold because someone on the roll call was missing. The most bestial and sadistic guards were assigned to that cell block. I was beaten bloody; I had running sores and was whipped, tortured; my food was cut in half; and I don't know to this day how I survived. Not many did.

"I lived out my punishment, and they sent me back to the bar-racks, where life was only another layer of the Inferno, but I remained alive, or rather one of the walking dead. In that horror and misery, suffering is the way life is, minute by minute, while the body, or the mind, deadens. Yes, so I suppose Wiesel is right. Even now, as I sit across from you and see you weeping, it comes back to me. I can only mouth words, and words cannot begin to tell you how it was. Nietzsche said that anything we can find words for is already dead in our hearts, that the very act of speaking produces a kind of contempt. And that is how I feel now.

"But no. Forget that. My contempt is not as Nietzsche meant, not for my experiences—they are not dead in my heart. My contempt is for the inadequacy of the words I must use.

"Feeling dead was not a constant. Fear could still take over. Hunger was always there, ready to drive one insane at any prospect of food, anything to prolong survival: the intensity of planning, the carrying out of a theft. My spirit could be lifted— lifted?—my entire self fulfilled at the gaining of something extra to eat, the smallest addition to my survival. Finding a rag to cover myself at night would elate my shrivelled being to bursting, if only for a moment. My reaction to the births of my children was pale beside my euphoria at gaining a pair of leather shoes that fit. I will not tell you how I gained them. I knew that my alternative was to choose death. I knew I lived beside men who were better than I, men who would have chosen to die before committing some of the actions of which I found myself capable. But no, after the cell-block, I had no choice. I had become nothing. As a Jew, I was one of the lowest. Maybe the homosexuals. Maybe they were tortured and died as we did, although there were homosexual guards, as I well knew.

"And then, before the year was out, some of us Jews who were left were let go. Simply let out. I can hardly understand to this day how I was given other clothes to put on, then found myself outside, where someone picked me up in a truck. I can't recall who it was— maybe it was just some person passing by—and he dropped me off near Erfurt. From there I made my way home after someone gave me enough money for a bus—I didn't have the wherewithal to beg. People walked past me and looked away, but some good person, an ordinary workman with a plain, honest German potato face, asked if I needed help, was I sick, and I said I had to get home, and he gave me...He didn't give me money, he gave me his sandwich and bought my ticket for me. I wolfed down the sandwich, and it was sitting heavily in my stomach, but I wanted more. I made myself concentrate on getting home and got on the bus. Someone behind me murmured to her friend that I must have cancer, and I turned around and said no, I was just released from a prison camp at Buchenwald, and everyone looked away. Because I am a Jew, I said. No one would answer or look at me. A young girl getting off at Apolda gave me an orange as she passed by, and I peeled it, I made myself peel it. I felt that if I could control my hunger, I'd regain something of myself. I ate that orange segment by segment. You can't imagine its taste.

"You can't imagine my mother's face when she saw me.

"You've heard of Herschel Grynszpan? That so-called assassination? This torture and imprisonment was before the war, an early action, a political action against Jews because of Herschel Grynszpan. And then it was over, for a time, except we knew what the government was capable of doing. Survivors knew, and so did our families. Those people on the bus, those Germans. They knew too.

"My father had escaped the pogrom by hiding out at the house of the friend they were visiting in the country, a gentile. But we knew we would all be rounded up next time, if not for a camp, for a ghetto. It was only a matter of time before all Jews would end up in camps. Women would not be spared. I had heard things, and seen what they did to young boys, and I knew now what internment would be like.

"That sandwich and orange almost killed me. But after a few days of my mother's care, I could tell my horror stories, and my parents and I tried to think of ways to leave Germany, the three of us. But they were not young. They were in their late thirties when I was born. My mother had arthritis, wasn't well enough to face the physical difficulties of escape, and it would be all for nothing at any rate as we were not well off. We could barely put together food for travel, let alone save for bribes and all it would take to cross a border. I found out later that other Jewish families had managed for their sons and husbands to be released if they, the whole family, agreed to leave the country. Once arrangements were made to leave and their property confiscated, the releases were put into effect. But my parents had heard nothing of this. They knew nothing and had no money. I think I was released because I was mistaken for someone, maybe somebody who was already dead.

"I'm going fast now, but I must tell you this as simply as possible. My parents made a terrible decision not to hold me back from leaving, from escaping Germany. After weeks of looking after me, seeing that I would live, they committed suicide one night by jumping off a high bridge near our neighbourhood. I found a note on their bed in the morning.

"But once they were gone, it was true: I was free. I was twenty years old and free.

"I knew without a doubt the brutality I had experienced would become widespread and that I had to get out of the country. Denmark was the only possibility. Switzerland was too far to the south and had indicated anyway it didn't want more Jewish immigrants, and at that time Denmark was not yet under Nazi rule.

"My father had inherited a piece of land east of Hamburg that we hadn't been able to get to for years, an isolated plot in a beech forest, with a tiny garden house that was nothing but a shed and a neglected garden. As a child, I had spent weeks there with my father on holiday, tending vegetables, picking berries, tramping the woods. Now it was illegal for Jews to own property, but a friend of my father, the same one who'd sheltered him, had taken it over in his name, though he had no interest in it. I thought if I made my way there I could hide long enough to prepare myself for the journey across the border. There would be rabbits and pheasants to snare or hunt with a slingshot, garden onions, asparagus, maybe some self-seeded tomatoes, potatoes. Yes. You could say I escaped one Buchenwald to find sanctuary in another.

"Escaping into the country was not yet impossible. My parents' German neighbours didn't know I was home. The ones on both sides of us were at work during the day and must have assumed that my parents killed themselves after hearing of my death. The police, who knows?

"I knew I had to leave right away. I packed a few tools and utensils, what little money there was, what food I could carry. It was 2 a.m., a warm night, but I wore my father's work coat with everything in the pockets, like Harpo Marx, and I took off for the north. When I saw myself in a shop window, I took the coat off, tied it all together, and shouldered it with the sleeves around my neck, like a pack. No one was about but the odd patrolman. Whenever I saw anyone, I hid. It took me all night to go ten blocks, and just before the daylight came, I ran behind a slow-moving farm truck with a tarp supported by a frame sheltering who knew what. At a stop sign, I managed to climb up, sneak under the cover, and there I found three pigs. Yes, three little pigs and I, no wolf. I remained still, and they settled down. I rode with them out of town and thought if the driver headed the wrong direction I could jump out once he slowed at a crossroads, but he turned north. My luck held because eventually he stopped at a farm and went inside the house without lifting the tarp to check on his animals. I was able to jump out and run into the woods a few dozen metres away and wait until night. Then I walked.

"I travelled only at night, weak and sometimes hallucinating. Once, I was walking along a deserted road when there appeared an oasis ahead of me, a garden with such vegetables—cucumbers thicker than watermelons, asparagus tall as trees, gigantic carrots with their orange tops straining from the earth. All lit up bright as day. I had the idea it was my father's garden in the forest, that I had made it there, but the sight faded, and I was again walking in darkness, half asleep.

"During the day I hid in mouldy haystacks, in closets in derelict buildings, burying myself in earth. I carried a small hatchet, and one morning I could find nowhere to hide—the countryside was flat farmland—so I loosened earth with the hatchet and hollowed out a shallow grave in a turnip field. I awakened to the taste of earth, terrified, but then realized where I was with such relief you cannot imagine—I was chilled and suffering from hunger and illness, but I was outdoors, alone, not in Buchenwald. Such a deliverance, the greatest joy. To this day I awaken like this from dreams of the camp.

"I have already gone on long enough. My escape through Schleswig-Holstein to Denmark is of no interest. My story is over. Yes, yes, I've talked about my trek across the Danish border many times—you can ask Simone, my daughter. Suffice to say, I made it there, and in 1940 the Nazis conquered Denmark, a peaceful takeover—the Danes wouldn't have had a chance had they resisted, and I was settled in Copenhagen and had learned to speak the language. As a German, I couldn't get a work permit, but I was able to stay under the radar. I lived in the basement suite of a couple who just asked for what rent I could give them from working at odd jobs. In '43 I escaped to Sweden with the Danish Jews and found employment with a landscaper.

"In the end I emigrated here because Louise, my wife, was from Saskatchewan. I met her in Berlin, where I went after the war when I decided to leave Europe altogether, maybe for Israel, but fate intervened. She was a Red Cross nurse.

"I was careful at first, even here in Canada, not to advertise I was a Jew, until I was given grief one day in the bar for being German. I gave a speech to the assemblage. Maybe I'd had too much to drink. I embarrassed them. At any rate, no one bothered me after that. And here, learning to farm, I gained some peace. This harsh land, the cold in winter, the heat of summer sun, burnt and froze some of my pain. The matter-of-fact life here, the elemental concerns of growing grain, raising some livestock. I was too busy, too concerned with making a living to reflect heavily on my past.

"I always leaned on my wife for companionship, moral support, but I in turn didn't supply much for her. She had to rely on women friends and neighbours, but she always accepted that, expected it I suppose. I was a reliable-enough husband and a decent father. Not a good one, but decent. As a husband, I don't know now—I suppose reliable was not all that she needed. Nietzsche says it is not the lack of love but a lack of friendship that makes unhappy marriages. But then, who is he to say, he himself who was so lacking success with other people? Ach, I am tired now, beginning to ramble. Why should I recall quotes from Nietzsche, whose words the Nazis twisted for themselves? But he was the one I studied most during my few student days.

"But now. There is one last thing. I don't have the strength left today, so I am asking you to come back. I will call you when I'm ready. There is something—I feel now I must tell the truth about something I have tried all my life to forget. You have shown up, it seems to me, almost out of nowhere, to listen, and I would like you to give me one more afternoon. I must finish with this. I lied to you about a great sin, a crime I committed. I am not a religious person. If there is a God, he is merely a creator with no morals, good or evil: he couldn't care less. But now that I am hurtling toward that good night, as the poet calls it, I want to confess.

TEN

She drives home carefully, consciously noting oncoming traffic and the angle of the sun on her windshield. Once, her mother-in-law, late one night over brandy in a rare moment of serious recollection, talked about the time just after the war. A teenager separated from her parents and desperate to escape Russian soldiers occupying Berlin, Renata had walked almost one hundred kilometres in one go to her home town.

"How could you keep on walking all that distance without sleep?" Lisa asked her.

"Terror," Renata said. She had reached her parents' house to find her mother alone. The Soviets were there too, and her father had been arrested, the Russians now using a recently vacated concentration camp for their German prisoners.

Lisa's own parents have been dead for well over a decade now, her dad fourteen years ago and her mom a couple of years later, but it doesn't seem that long ago. She wants her mother. A particular memory of them often comes to her, an image cast in nostalgia and the soft light of the floor lamp in their living room, of her mother sitting on the couch between her husband and son-in-law looking at an old photo album of baby pictures.

"Lisa," she said, turning to Gerhardt, "she had such a kissable neck."

Gerhardt said, "She still does," and her dad laughed. The three of them turned to look at her, teasing. Such a small memory, but it has the weight of an icon; the moment defines something about her. *I was gently raised.* She wonders how she will deal with the rest of Ben Meisner's story and feels sick at the prospect of more knowledge.

··

THAT TIME IN LONDON, on her last day at O.E. Nunn and Co., during afternoon tea and cigarettes, Mr. Wilkes said, "I killed a man once."

"I beg your pardon?"

"During the war."

"Oh." She felt a mixture of relief and disappointment. Since when, she wondered, had she begun to say I beg your pardon?

"You don't understand," he said. "He was a German prisoner and unarmed. He was about the same distance from me as you are now, and I shot him." He seemed intent upon having Lisa comprehend something he knew was beyond her. "I was marching him to prison camp over the Yorkshire moors. An airman. We'd captured him about ten miles across country, and I was to take him to the camp."

Mr. Wilkes looked intently at his hands and tapped his fingers together. They were so tobacco-stained they blended in with the desk. "We walked about six or seven miles through the heather. It was blooming purple. We stopped at a tiny place with a call box and I contacted headquarters. They told me they had bad news then. They told me my brother had been killed in France. So I went outside and shot the German."

"Good lord," Lisa said.

"Aye," said Mr. Wilkes. "Good lord." He seemed satisfied then. Not because he'd managed to present his story to her, but because he still recalled the event with satisfaction. She hadn't ever heard him say aye before.

••

SHE TURNS DOWN the gravel road leading to her place, carefully noting the dust of a vehicle in the distance. Why would she conjure up other people's stories right now? Is she comparing? That would be ridiculous. Suffering—that of her mother-in-law, Mr. Wilkes, the man he murdered—could be comprehended. But something like Buchenwald's punishment block: she could only imagine something surreal, something out of Bosch.

At home, finding herself staring at a blank wall in her kitchen, she pours a drink from the last of the vodka. After one sip, she puts the glass down and starts to pace, plagued by an energy she doesn't know how to expend. Her bones want to jump through her skin. Without thinking about it, she hauls out the vacuum cleaner, goes over the carpets and couch, sweeps and damp-mops the hardwood floors, grabs a dust rag and Pledge instead of the usual fake feather duster and sprays and polishes all the furniture, then scours the kitchen and bathrooms.

Resting on the couch late that night, she sips the rest of her vodka and tonic, so flat and watered down by now she can taste nothing but a hint of bitterness. Admiring her immaculate living room, she realizes she hasn't cleaned the house this quickly and thoroughly in years, if ever. That must indicate something positive. Maybe since she is going through what used to be called "the change," she might actually be changing. Tomorrow she will tackle the windows, make them shine, give them high-def transparency.

••

SHE SETS UP the stepladder outside and works her way from window to window with a washrag and a bucket of water and vinegar, polishing with newspaper. She wipes off a dusty film that she estimates has been building up for four years. Gerhardt's mother would be shocked. No German would be caught dead with four years' worth of grime on their windows. Her Aunt Gemma used to say, "Clean all the corners, and the centre will take care of itself." Yes. She will go over the entire house from the bottom up.

After finishing the windows inside, she goes down to the basement, which hasn't ever been cleaned except for a bit of sweeping when they moved in. Wiping down the storage shelves just off the furnace room, she comes across a large plastic bag full of cotton cleaning rags she'd added to for years but then forgotten. Just what she needs.

She wonders if hiding a person down here would be possible. Maybe a couple of people could sleep behind the cupboard doors if the shelves were removed. They could play cards and eat at the table she uses to fold laundry.

Wiping the shelves and their supply of cans and Kraft Dinner, she finds an unopened bottle of Kahlúa in a back corner. It must be left over from the previous owners, unless Gerhardt hid a secret stash. But if he stashed anything it would be scotch or vodka. She sets it aside and goes back to washing away a decade or two of dust and spiderwebs. She pulls another plastic bag from the back of a dusty shelf and finds the old SS coat Gerhardt brought from Germany, its grey leather looking new against the crinkled white plastic. Gerhardt. He couldn't bring himself to throw away something of such good quality. She unfolds the overcoat to its full length on the laundry table, the leather gleaming under the basement light bulb. She examines the worn satin lining, the large zippered pocket that would have held the officer's valuables. On a white tag, the word *Robe* is embroidered, with the right leg of the R extending in a horizontal line under *ein Qualitätsbegriff*, with the names *J. Rosenberger* and *M. Gladbach.* Rosenberger sounds Jewish. Could that be possible? *Ein Qualitätsbegriff.* An idea of quality. What should that translate as, really? An image of quality? The very image of quality. She considers it for a long moment before folding it up and returning it to its place on the shelf. She thinks of Gogol's *The Overcoat.* Gogol wasn't Jewish, was he?

She wonders if Ben Meisner, feeding the cattle on a winter morning, ever regretted not emigrating to Israel. A memory from her own trip to Israel flashes as bright as a vision: orange peels left in the ashes of a campfire in the desert by the Red Sea, their colour still vibrant but dried so brittle by the end of the day that they burned as well as the few sticks of wood she and Gerhardt had managed to scrape together.

Upstairs, she dusts off the Kahlúa bottle and wonders how old it is, if it would be safe to try out. She pours some of the brown syrup over ice and tastes it. Good. She adds milk, then a bit more liqueur until it is a creamy chocolate colour. A reward for cleaning the corners, she thinks as she savours the sweetness and feels warmth slip through her veins. Walking to the kitchen table, she notices her jeans let off little clouds of dust. She will finish the drink, then have a bath, have another Kahlúa and milk, and watch *Jeopardy* in her spotless living room.

··

SHE HAS NEVER before in her life washed walls—she always found it less effort and more effective to paint over dirt. She empties the bag of rags she found in the basement onto her kitchen table: old shirts ripped apart at the seams; Tyler's worn-out Superman pyjamas; a black T-shirt of Stephanie's with embroidered spiders and butterflies; worn flannel and brushed cotton sheets cut into big, soft squares; and the khaki remains of her old Israeli army shirt.

The living room, office, and bedrooms need a mere once-over, but the kitchen is satisfyingly difficult. With its film of grease, the ceiling is nearly impossible, yet she perseveres. Section by section, it takes up most of the next day. The thick cotton of the army jacket holds up well. Her arms aching, she thinks of the energy, the toughness she associated with the Israelis she met. Maybe the heat and sun, the militant self-reliance of its people helped cleanse some of the detritus of the Holocaust. Cleanse. Ethnic cleansing. What an innocuous term for mass slaughter.

On another of the Israeli beaches—was it near Eilat too? No, it was somewhere by the Mediterranean—Gerhardt put his hand on her sun-warmed back and said, "Lisa. Look out past the pier." She sat up, sleepily put on her sunglasses, and saw Tweedledum and Tweedledee. Identical middle-aged twins were sitting, one on either side of an inner tube, each an exact reflection of the other: bald heads circled by brownish-grey fringes, bellies like red beach balls forcing the inner tube under the water, round faces grinning gleefully. They floated around and around, moving slowly away from the crowd of swimmers, reminding her of hippo ballerinas in a cartoon. She saw the twins again later, lying flat on their backs on matching blankets with towels covering their eyes. They spoke English with Eastern European accents, chatting loudly as people do when they can't see each other, their voices distinct among the beach clamour. "It was Long Island tea," one of them said. "What?" asked the other. "The name of that drink I was talking about." As she walked past, she noticed numbers tattooed on their wrists. She did not point them out to Gerhardt.

She finds rubbing alcohol and an old toothbrush in the bathroom and cleans all the light switches and plug-ins in the house. She takes the lamp shades outside on the steps to dust off with a baby's hairbrush. She sets the houseplants on the grass and sprays each one with a mild soap solution, then rinses with the hose set on mist. She cleans the TV remote control, the telephones, and the computer keyboard. She eyes the alcohol bottle, still half full, and sniffs it contemplatively. What would this stuff taste like mixed with cranberry juice? Just joking, she assures herself. She just needs to take a drive to the liquor store. Besides, there is some Kahlúa left.

••

SHE IS RELIEVED to be called about a teaching job in P.A. A social studies teacher has twisted an ankle, the principal tells her Friday evening, and will be out of commission for a couple of days. At least they've given her adequate notice this time. She could get up on Monday expecting to go to work like a normal person.

The empty classroom holds an unusual, rather pleasant scent. Lemon, is it? But mixed with some sort of chemical. The industrial floor tile shines newly polished, and she realizes the smell is old-fashioned floor wax. Her spirits lift; she feels as if the room has been prepared for her. She is glad to be subbing in a high school today, to be able to put on something other than the casual pants and Hush Puppies she wears for dealing with younger kids. Feeling professional in her business clothes, gratified by the friendliness of the teachers in the staff room, she thinks how good it is to have gainful employment once in a while, to be part of the real world. Maybe she should look for something more permanent.

Her first class is grade eleven history. As she examines the register, she realizes she knows some of these kids—she spent time with them last year covering for a math teacher with the flu, trying to fake some competence in grade ten algebra. She wasn't very successful, but none of the students cared, or noticed for that matter.

This teacher has prepared in-class work that Lisa is only to supervise, and the students are assigned a chapter to read with questions to answer after they finish. She could promote discussion toward the end if she felt so inclined. She'll decide what to do once she's read the chapter herself. It is about the Red River Rebellion.

From the hallway, sounds of arriving students begin to invade the peace. She puts on her teaching expression—friendly, a bit wry and willing to be amused, but with that hint of toughness making it obvious she won't put up with any shit. She has tried to perfect it over the years, along with a matching tone of voice. Today it seems to require more effort than usual.

The boys who straggle in sport the usual two distinct fashions. One group has hippie-ish long hair but wears jeans hip-hop style, sagging to feature their boxer shorts, frayed cuffs dragging on the floor. The other group comes across as jock-ish, with ordinary T-shirts and jeans and short hair, some with actual buzz cuts. The girls are harder to read. Their jeans all have low waists, T-shirts are all tight, even on the girls whose figures could use something looser. She supposes she could divide them into those who wear a lot of eye makeup and those who don't.

She gets up to write her name and remains standing. "Some of you might remember me," she says. "Mrs. Braun?"—she waves to indicate the board—"And I'll be here until Mrs. Nicholson's ankle is better."

"Brawn, like the razor blade?" The voice comes from a lanky track star she recognizes from last year, lounging at the back of the room.

"Yes." She tries to inject several meanings into the one word, and the accompanying steely gaze. He subsides, grinning. God, she thinks, feeling her optimism seep away. All the energy teachers have to expend just to glean a few grains of common courtesy. She outlines the assignment. She watches the students turn the pages of their textbooks docilely enough, one or two taking notes. They remember her. She's already done some groundwork here and can relax a bit.

She pages through the text along with the class, but another teaching unit catches her eye, about World War II. Stephanie and Tyler studied the Holocaust in grade eleven; maybe this is the same textbook, updated. A chapter in the war unit features a selection of memories of Canadian and American soldiers interspersed with those of prisoners of war. The first memory is that of a Jewish woman captured in Italy, who told of being forced to slog through the mud on a road toward the French border, carrying her baby. A German soldier, passing by with a troop going the other direction, stopped to help her over a barrier. "Try to hold on until you reach Germany," he said. "In our country we don't treat women and children this way."

She puts the book down and wonders about that soldier, what he thought he was fighting for. She recalls her mother-in-law, after *Schindler's List* came out, watching a news report about American audiences cheering the deaths of German soldiers in the movie. "To stand up and cheer!" She'd been upset and disgusted. "Most of them were only boys. They were soldiers at war, just like the British or Americans."

Lisa gazes out at the class. These boys are old enough to have been drafted in Germany back then, at least toward the end of the war. Some of them slouch and look off into space, some read. Although a few of them look Métis themselves, none seem too interested in the Red River Rebellion. A girl and a boy nod off over their desks, looking as if they might be on something. She puts that thought away.

She turns back to the chapter on World War II. The second excerpt is from the point of view of a young American soldier liberating a concentration camp.

We walked down a trail through the forest. The smell was over-powering before we even got there. Although I was only twenty years old, I'd seen a lot. But nothing prepared me for this. In the clearing, surrounded by barbed wire and low huts, was a pile of bodies stacked like cordwood. They were nothing but skeletons covered in skin turned a grey-green color. You could see they'd all been starved to death. And then from the other direction came a group of those who were not quite dead yet, walking like zombies. Skeletons wearing black-and-white stripes, each with the Star of David sewn on the shirt.

With no warning, she is struck by a sensation of heaviness. As if some agent of misery has decided to force her down, to focus right this moment on her sitting here, reading this. She feels that focus narrow onto the back of her neck. She concentrates on a yoga exercise: Breathe. Take breaths that seem to fill your abdomen instead of your lungs. The weight diminishes, enabling her to go back to the chapter they are all supposed to be reading. She lets the students take their time answering the written assignment.

That evening she feels compelled to look up the rest of the American soldier's memories on a website recommended with caution in the textbook. The article is accompanied by photographs.

Of course she has seen pictures before of the concentration camps. Everybody has seen these photos. But the split between the soldiers' viewpoints, this American and the German who took the decency of his country for granted, strikes her today with a new immediacy. It is as if the descriptions of the camp have infiltrated her being, and she, or some part of her, is inside, can almost smell, almost taste the rancid air. She is afraid to go to sleep.

But she has no nightmares, and she finishes the next day of her teaching stint with a certain bland competence. The morning after it is done, she makes coffee and sits down at the computer. She googles "holocaust memories" and finds dozens of websites. She watches survivors talk into the camera, recounting their experiences in every manner from stoic deadpan to heart-wrenching weeping. Some seem to find the telling liberating; some relive the horror so vividly she can see they are damaged all over again.

An ordinary-looking man, old, frail, silver-haired, with wire-rimmed glasses: He was caught trying to escape the country, he says. He was burnt with hot irons. His nails were pulled out. Electric shocks were administered to his genitals. He was interrogated and beaten by two special whippers who changed shifts, simply doing their day jobs. All this told in matter-of-fact language, looking straight into the camera. He and his words right there on the screen in front of her. She doesn't know what she is expected to do with them. What she expects.

Websites feature black-and-white photos, segments of film. A truckload of silently crying children tossed out like garbage, herded toward a cement bunker, guards' expressions grotesque from barking orders at four-year-olds, sorting out twins, the introduction says, for temporary survival. The guards' faces right there on YouTube for their grandchildren to see.

She thinks about the soldier in the school textbook who said "In our country we don't treat women and children so" and wonders how long it took for that young German to realize the truth. Wonders if it were possible, conceivable, for someone like him to become a guard like those in the film.

She continues searching until, sometime in the evening, she realizes she hasn't eaten anything all day.

ELEVEN

She has gone through various personal eras of questioning why, of reading about the Holocaust, but has never felt anything like this. She's always been able to keep some distance, has had to develop a certain pragmatic perspective, particularly given that part of her own heritage is German. How do people from Germany live with it? As far as she knows from Gerhardt's parents, they simply get on with their lives and refuse to remember. They encourage their children to acknowledge it happened but not to dwell on it, and that is probably the only way. World War II has long passed. It is in the past.

She recalls, years ago, longing to hear Peter Gzowski or any typical Canadian voice on the radio after the visit with Gerhardt's grandmother. How kind the grandmother was to her at the family gathering, painting that portrait of herself as a girl, choosing German phrases simple enough for Lisa to understand. She died in her sleep only a few months after they returned home. "We knew what to turn our backs to," she'd said.

Soon after the Wall came down, Lisa and Gerhardt and the kids made one of their trips to Germany. Gerhardt's parents were considering a move from Berlin back to their old village in the Eastern bloc, although Renata was hesitant. They'd escaped to

West Germany just before the Wall was built. Some of their old neighbours, those who would have turned them in if they'd known their plans, those who'd stolen what they'd left behind, were still living there. They would be there to deal with, to have to say hello to, all these years later. In the end, they compromised and found an apartment in a bigger town nearby.

But that summer day, before anything was decided, Renata and Karl took the four of them, along with Gerhardt's sister and her husband, on a day trip to their old village across the newly demolished border. They parked Peter's new SUV in the neighbourhood and walked across a bridge that reminded Stephanie and Tyler of the Billy Goats Gruff. They followed Karl past the house where he'd been born, past the house in which he and Renata had their first apartment after Karl returned home in 1945. He'd spent most of the war stationed in Norway. He said a lot of soldiers remained in Norway after the war, since the people were relatively friendly and conditions were so much better there than at home.

In the early nineties, West Germans were enthusiastically buying up East German property, restoring old buildings, the government fixing potholed roads and rotting structures. But Gelburg was still a grey East German village, ramshackle, with stucco falling off houses, cracks in sidewalks, the odd flock of geese in a backyard. The solidity, the absolute squareness of West German buildings, the Disney-like perfection of the restorations and renovations that were reclaiming the country as a whole again, none of it had conquered this village yet.

The side of the road, however, featured a series of new signs that cropped up at certain points. From a distance, Lisa could see only the black-and-white outlines of a symbolic person, a skeletal figure dressed in stripes. Had there been a concentration camp right there in the village? Gerhardt's family ignored the signs and

continued to walk on, pointing out the school and various important landmarks from their youth. Gerhardt herded Stephanie and
Tyler, who were in the half-aware state of preadolescents resigned
to an afternoon of boredom, farther down the street. Lisa trailed
off the path to examine one of the signs.

A heading said *Totemarch*. Death march. From what she can
remember of the text, it said that along this route walked thousands of Jews forced by the Nazis to march from prison camps
pointlessly to their deaths shortly before the end of the war. The
signs were there to memorialize the route as a tribute to those
who had suffered, and to remind Germans not to forget.

The cobblestones soaking up the hazy sunlight of that afternoon had been trodden by people in such misery she closed her
mind to it. She fell back in with her in-laws and their averted
faces. Gerhardt, walking ahead with the kids, pointed out a small
park where he used to play with a gang of friends.

He had long since closed the door on the Holocaust. And when,
after watching *Sophie's Choice*, Lisa had spent the remainder of the
evening weeping in the bathroom, they'd both wordlessly agreed
to avoid watching any more movies or documentaries about it. By
then Lisa, too, was sick of the subject. How could an entire society
either participate in or ignore such monstrous atrocity? Was it all
fear? She knew the banality of her questions, the universality of
her bewilderment. The whole world had been mystified, disgusted,
had condemned the German people to generations of atonement.

And now she thinks of Gerhardt's overprotective parenting, of
all the German *Papas* who are possessed by their families. Is this
what made the persecution of the Jews possible, she wonders?
Other people might be your own neighbours, but to Germans they
are always just that: other.

She has read Arendt and Goldhagen, Levi and Wiesel, and has imagined herself in scenarios in which she had choices. She has no idea if she would risk the detention and torture of her own family by daring to speak out. Would she have risked even the mere ostracizing, the social suffering of her children to protest against the suffering of Jewish children? Especially if she didn't know the extent of what was happening, what was going on in the camps? She likely wouldn't risk anything at all, even now.

A wave of heat consumes her so relentlessly it forces her out of the computer chair. She finds herself standing outside on the back deck, the cool spring air soothing like ice on a fever. The view from here is still a brown expanse broken by bare poplar and small spruce trees, the willow bushes down by the creek golden with sap and ready to leaf out. A birch tree Gerhardt saved by cutting down the poplars choking it stands outlined in stark white against the blue sky. She gazes at it, not moving, until she feels well chilled, like a carafe of white wine, she thinks; like the birch tree itself. A bit too cool now, she continues to stand, not wanting to break this pristine peace.

After a quick supper, she settles in front of the TV, ignoring the pull of the computer. She knows if she lets herself look up more websites, she'll be there all night. She switches the channel to her favourite talk show, lulled into the comfortable inanity of the jokes when the phone rings. An unlisted number. At ten at night? Gerhardt must be borrowing someone's phone. Or maybe it's Stephanie, calling from her boyfriend's cell phone. "Hello?"

"Mrs. Brawwn? At Box 96, Cullen, Saskatchewan?" The voice is nasal, female. A collection agent looking for Stephanie? Somebody requesting a donation?

"Who is this?"

"Statistics Canada calling, regarding the labour force survey you were notified about in the mail. Are you Lisa Braun at that address?" The caller is officious, insistent.

Caught off guard, she says yes, she is. "But I'm not interested in any survey."

"Participation in this survey is Required By Law."

Cowed by the sound of capital letters, she doesn't say anything. "It was all outlined," the woman continues, "in the literature we sent you. We will be calling you once a month for six months."

Literature? She hasn't picked up the mail in ages. Every month for six months? Not a chance. "I'm sorry, but we make it a rule not to respond to telephone solicitors." It is what she tells anyone like this who phones. If she hadn't been taken by surprise, she would have said it right away and hung up. "And that includes soliciting information," she adds.

"Ma'am. This survey is required. By law." The woman's voice sharpens. "Now, this will just take a few minutes. How many working adults live at your address?"

Lisa senses this is legitimate, that only a civil servant could sound this officious at this time of night. But she says, "How do I know who you are? Who would phone this late, showing an unlisted number?"

"You didn't answer any of our previous calls."

She remembers disconnecting several 1-800 numbers as usual, and thinking that lately there did seem to be more junk calls. She lets silence float over the line, not quite able to hang up.

"I'll give you a number to call," the woman finally says.

Another 800 number. But she copies it down before she hangs up. What does "required by law" mean? That police would show up at her door? The sound of jackboots on her steps. "Open up in the name of the law!" A Kafkaesque judge in a wig pounding his gavel: For refusing to co-operate with Statistics Canada, you are hereby sentenced to seven years of hard labour.

Aw, shit. She presses the TV sound back on. She's missed the best part of the show, and now there's nothing but a nervous starlet expecting to be humiliated. She turns it off. Bullies are everywhere. That woman on the phone would probably go home tonight and kick her dog, or tell her daughter she is too fat.

She wishes their dog, Woofer, were still around. He was such a quiet, comforting old thing, his presence assuring her everything was fine as long as he was awake and watching. They'd inherited the easygoing collie–lab cross along with the property, and he'd welcomed his new owners as if he were the host and she and Gerhardt guests. Woofer would accompany them on walks, allow himself to be scratched and petted, would fetch the odd stick if he were feeling especially gracious. He didn't seem unhappy but pre-occupied, as if he wondered where his real family was but accepted her and Gerhardt as better than nothing. They would do in the dark, as her Aunt Gemma would say. Woofer died of old age as unobtrusively as he'd lived, and they decided not to get another dog. Whenever they went away, it was for too long; they didn't want to have to worry.

She looks up the Statistics Canada website. Yes, participation in the labour survey is required. They want answers about the jobs of people in your household, hours worked, salaries, sick days. None of it is any of their business, and they certainly have no business regularly wasting her time over six months. "Penalty for Noncompliance: Five hundred dollars and/or three months in jail." And/or. Well, she would see about that. She would phone that number and complain.

By the time she punches in the StatsCan phone number the next morning, she has made up her mind she's done all she can in the house. She will start work on her garden. At least she can go outside and check out the paths, see if she needs to buy more wood chips. But first she will complain. A woman's voice answers the phone. Lisa tells her she is outraged at being telephoned late at night and threatened with time in jail if she refuses to participate in something that is essentially a telemarketing survey. The woman is very sorry but the survey is compulsory, just like the census. This voice, soothing, accommodating, says no information would be provided to anyone outside Statistics Canada. She says Lisa doesn't have to reply to any questions she feels uncomfortable answering, doesn't even have to provide her name. Lisa says she is uncomfortable answering anything at all. The woman apologizes for them bothering her late in the evening, that will never happen again, but, she suggests calmly, why don't they just do the first interview right now, while she is already on the line.

Lisa knows she is being placated and manipulated but gives up. Is it worth it to risk having to go to court, pay a fine? She confirms her address, provides her and her husband's ages, removes their names. The phrase "What's the use?" crosses her mind in an almost audible chant.

"What is your occupation?"

She is about to answer when she catches her reflection in the newly polished coffee table, noticing with satisfaction the soft gleam of hardwood around the vacuumed area rug. "Housewife," she says.

"Okay, so you're not in the workforce?"

She pretends to be insulted. "I'll have you know my work is as valuable as anyone's."

After a beat, the voice forges ahead. "That's certainly correct, but you're not earning a salary. You work inside the home. Now the adult male of your household. What is his occupation?"

"Gardener," she hears herself say with no hesitation at all. A slight shock travels through her nervous system, as if she has touched someone after dragging her feet. Then she thinks gardener might be too vague, might invite more questions. "Horticulturist, and designs landscapes in the off-season." She makes up the number of hours worked last week. Hours of overtime. Time missed because of illness. Company he works for? Himself, she decides. Income? She has no clue. "I don't feel comfortable answering questions about our finances."

"All right." The voice grants her that, and wraps up the interview.

••

SHE ACCESSES the Holocaust websites again, sits up late reading or listening to people weave hideous memories into a fabric of nightmares. She keeps looking and looking, somehow can't quit. For the first time, she brings herself to search for one of Mengele's child victims.

I'd just turned eleven and had been in Auschwitz for several weeks when I was torn from my older sisters and lined up with other children. These little twins, Etta and Golda, who I tried to take some care of because they wouldn't stop crying, were holding onto my hands. Mengele told his assistant to pull the three of us out of the queue and take us to the lab, where I saw bed after bed of children screaming in pain, bloody and tortured, some gagged. The two little girls were stripped and tied down, injected with something. I cried out and fell to my knees. I was slapped across the face and then tied down on a bed on the other side of the room and cut with scalpels. I never saw those little girls again. I was left alone and in pain for hours. I was whipped. I was starved and tortured every

day. They force fed me with drugs that made me sick. I was
punctured with needles and tubes until there was no space
left on my body. The scalpels were dirty and they let the
wounds fester so they could study them…

..

ENOUGH. SHE IS horrified and disgusted, partly with herself. Sitting
there comfortably at her computer, reading this. She becomes
aware of something pulling at her. Gravity. She finds it impossible to sit any longer, but neither does it seem possible to stand,
so she kneels beside the computer. She thinks of the uselessness
of prayer, more words in a vacuum, and lies on the floor, flat on
her back. She notices roller marks on the ceiling. If Gerhardt is so
German in other ways, why has he never embraced perfection-
ism? A job well done? She turns her head to the side, watches
dust balls under the desk dance to an inaudible tune. What did
Aunt Gemma call them? Slut's wool. She sits up. Speaking of
vacuums. She will put off doing the garden. She has to clean, all
over again.

That night she can't sleep until after dawn. It's almost noon
before she has the energy to start her day. In spite of her intention
to leave it alone, she is turning on the computer when the phone
rings, another unfamiliar number. She considers letting it ring,
but answers.

"Hi, Mom."

"Oh! Stephanie! How are you?"

"Pretty good."

"It's good to hear your voice," she says.

"You sound kind of weird, Mom. Are you okay?"

"I…Well. Yes, I guess so."

She has a quick memory of Stephanie aged eight or nine in the dentist's chair, the dentist saying his assistant is about to give her a fluoride treatment that will make her drool. At home they'd been teasing Tyler and Gerhardt, girls rule and boys drool, and the word struck both of them as so funny they had a giggling fit right there, the dentist grinning in the bewildered way of people who don't get the joke but would like to.

"I've been realizing how much I miss you," she says, tears gathering in her voice.

"Really?" Stephanie's voice holds a hint of suspicion.

"Yes." She makes a quick decision. "I'm feeling, uh…I'd like to talk. Not about any of our, whatever. Issues. It's just that I've been sort of depressed since Dad went up north, and I need to talk to someone who might understand."

"Oh? *Really*?"

"Well, you…" She almost gives in to irritation, almost says, Well you don't have to sound so astonished. "Remember when you did all that research on the Holocaust, when you were about fifteen or sixteen?"

"Yes? Well, like, that was a long time ago."

"I did some volunteering at the seniors' complex, in town here? I got to know this old man who's a survivor of Buchenwald. He told me his story, and it got me looking up even more information, on the computer."

Stephanie clears her throat, hesitating. "Oh?"

"So now I'm sort of, uh…obsessed. I mean, it's horribly depressing, but I can't seem to stop looking things up. I thought since you went through a time in your own life when you were reading the same sort of thing, maybe felt a bit the same way, we might be able to talk about it." She feels she is babbling.

After a moment, Stephanie says, "I don't know what to say. That was such a long time ago, and I've avoided thinking about it since then. I just, like, quit I guess. I'm 90 percent German, you know—there's not much I can do about it."

"You're not 90 percent."

"Whatever."

"So, you think I should just quit."

"No. Like, I know it's not that simple." She pauses. "Dad told me once he went through thinking about it a lot too, as a teenager. He said you have to decide."

"Decide what?"

"Well, to live or not. Not live with it, but to live. There's no understanding, no coming to terms with it, so you have to leave it alone."

"Did your research back then have anything to do with your turning to drugs?" She can't help herself.

"My turning to drugs." Stephanie gives an audible sigh. "You know what? I've told you this already, and I don't know what you want to hear. Just—I'm not strung out, Mom. I'm doing okay."

"Good. I'm glad."

"I didn't start to do drugs because of any one thing. I got into smoking weed at Jennifer's place. She always had a stash, and like, her parents didn't mind."

"Jennifer? Whose place you always ran off to? You certainly never told me that before."

"Then I met Josh. I wasn't... I never was any more traumatized about anything than anyone else was. I researched the Holocaust because I was, like, pissed off at everything. At you and Dad. I don't even know why. I wasn't, uh... Of course it was depressing, but I found it affirming in a weird way. Well, you know what I was like."

"No, I don't really."

"Affirming my black view of the universe. Ha. How low people can go."

"Do you still have a black view of the universe?"

"Oh, I don't know. Sometimes."

When she isn't high, Lisa thinks. An abrupt sense of futility takes away any urge to talk, and now she doesn't know what else to say.

After a moment, Stephanie says, "So, like, I was calling because I lost my old cell, and now I need Dad's phone number again."

"You mean Caribou Point School?"

"Yeah, that, and his cell number too."

She gives out the numbers. "You know there's no cell phone service up there?"

"Yes, I know, but just so I have it. Uh, Mom? Are you okay?" She sounds vague, dutiful. "Is there...I mean, like, if you want, we can talk."

"No. Of course I have to deal with this on my own. I don't know what I was thinking. Even if I discussed every detail of what I'm going through, which I can't really put into words anyway, it wouldn't do any good. I can always phone Dad to come home for a while if I really need to."

"Okay." They are both silent until Stephanie signs off. "Well, bye then, love you."

"Me too."

She sits for another minute at her computer, the phone still in her hand. She turns off the screen without looking at it but is gripped by such weariness she has to wait a moment before she can stand up. Once she does, she goes to bed for a nap.

TWELVE

She is about to be shot. She is standing in line, naked, with other naked people who are pale, flabby, as ordinary as herself, waiting. Jack Cennon, a radio and TV personality from her childhood, is there to interview her, but he can only get as close as the outer periphery of barbed wire. He is calling out questions she can't understand. She is next in line, frozen with horror, when she wakes up to an afternoon cacophony of crows and sparrows. The dream was so vivid she can't believe she is lying safe in her own bed. She lies stiff, unable to move for several minutes.

Sunlight illuminates the bedroom, highlighting each fold of blanket, each curve of furniture. The crows in the spruce trees croak a raucous celebration of life. Sparrows chirp arias just outside her window. Getting up to look out, she sees that every tree and plant, even an old pair of boots left on the back deck, is finely delineated into beauty like a Mary Pratt painting, everything outlined in relief.

She is ravenous. She'd hasn't eaten much for days, and now cooks an early supper, or late lunch, of comfort food: Kraft Dinner and beans, each Agent-Orange-covered macaroni a neon miracle, each bean a brown oval of benediction. She makes coffee the German way, dark and strong, and goes outside with her cup to enjoy the dazzling spring light.

Shrub and poplar branches trace intricate patterns against the dark green of spruce trees. Heads of dried feather reed grass wave in the breeze beside round grey seedheads of globe thistle, chocolate pods of coneflowers. The leftover beauty is so soothing she is sorry it's time to cut everything back, to rake it all up to make room for new growth.

She notes that the front garden is dry now. Usually by this time of year the garden is an obsession; it's housekeeping she has to force herself to do. She goes inside for more coffee. Through pristine windows she inspects a cloudless sky and the garden, waiting for her.

Arming herself with a rake and clippers, she starts with the delphiniums, their thick, hollow spikes the toughest to deal with, and hopes this year there will be no fat green worms festering in any of the flower buds. She straightens up to stretch, still a bit stiff from the day she cleaned the ceiling. She feels a magnetic prickle between her shoulder blades as if someone is watching her, but she puts that notion away.

The sky shimmers a cobalt blue. The lilac shrubs sheltering the garden look skeletal; they are growing gangly, in need of a trim. They connect up with wild bush on the west side, where a small stand of willows and black poplar covers a boggy depression fronted by spruce, scrub pine, and aspens, all competing with tangled underbrush. The leafless trees remind her of her dream. Telling herself it is ridiculous, she continues to sense that the bush harbours something, or somebody, watching her. Keeping to the other side of the plot, she clears the Maltese crosses, false sunflowers, globe thistles, goldenrod, and daylilies, all the tough sun-lovers she gleaned from Aunt Gemma's old garden. Gemma is now over ninety and, since her stroke, lives in a seniors' place in Regina, close to her sons. The last time Lisa visited, Gemma didn't recognize her.

Standing up to admire the growing pile of stalks, she allows herself a grain of satisfaction. She surveys the yard: the vegetable plot is still too wet to dig, and she'll have to add more wood chips to the paths this year. The sunlight warms the top of her head; the air is mild if a bit clammy. Starting in on stalks nearer to the bush, she admires the trees bursting with sap, pines and spruce aromatic as car fresheners, willow branches golden, aspens glowing with life, their leaves almost ready to come out. Green stems are already concealed among most of the perennials. Her lily and peony beds were cleared into neat black arcs back in the fall as Lois Hole, her favourite garden writer, advised. She would consult all her gardening books again.

She gathers the pile of dead stems to throw in the compost, wondering absently if before her wedding Mrs. Hole had any thoughts about keeping her maiden name, when she hears something. She stands up straight and still to listen. She can hear a definite rustling and snapping noise. It isn't her imagination. Something is there, in the bush, maybe twenty feet away, heavy enough to crack twigs and branches underfoot. A bear? Just out of hibernation, and hungry. One of the spruce trees begins to shake, raining dead needles and old cones. She knows she should run but stands frozen until a head the size of a softball, suspended in the evergreen like a Disney Christmas ornament, with a comically oversized flat beak and large dark eyes, peers at her. Then its neck snakes out from behind the branches, followed by a feathered oil-barrel of a body. An ostrich stands outlined against the dark green boughs, its scaly yellow legs matching the willow branches. She and the bird gaze at each other in stupid astonishment.

No. Of course it isn't an ostrich, it's one of Robbie Danielson's emus, escaped. "You," she says to the thing. "You almost gave me a heart attack." She turns her back on it, drops her armful of debris, and goes in to phone Robbie. He and Marjorie have a couple of emus left from a herd of fifty they'd built up until ten years ago, when they had to get rid of them because there was no market. They are able to break even on the feed for the two they keep by selling eggs and feathers to a crafts co-op in Saskatoon.

It's Saturday, Robbie says, so he can send the twins over on the quads to chase it home. Within ten minutes, the youngest Danielson kids arrive on all-terrain vehicles, carrying lariats. She is surprised to see two gangly teenagers; it can't be more than a few months ago that they were freckled and cute. Each sits on what looks like a cross between a motorbike and a miniature jeep, looking around for the bird until she opens the door and waves at them. "It must have gone back in the bush," she calls, pointing as if they could miss it. Leaving the motors running, they tramp, in an exaggerated skulk for her benefit, into the trees to flush it out. She listens to the cracked hilarity in their voices and shakes her head. They are growing up. The bird crashes through the underbrush into the yard, where it circles crazily, then heads straight down the driveway to the road. Whooping, the boys jump on their vehicles and tear after it. They shouldn't be driving on the grid road, she thinks, but she isn't about to tell on them.

At any rate, here is Robbie himself, driving up in his half-ton just in time to watch the slapstick. Now she'll have to make conversation. She waves as he hefts himself casually out of his truck. "Come on in," she says, trying to unearth some heartiness. "I'll put the coffee on."

He was good-looking and rather wild in his youth, Marjorie once told her, and she could see how that might have been true. In spite of his bulk, he has never lost a certain confidence of move-ment, that straight-backed strut of favoured country boys. He is shaking his head in half-amused exasperation. "Goddamned little clowns'll scare the bugger to death." He doesn't seem too worried.

They sit at the kitchen table. "So I hear Ger's left you again," he says jocularly.

"Yep," she agrees. "A whole school term up in Caribou Point. The Gulag, he calls it."

He grins. "You'd better watch out, he might get addicted to the North." He reaches for his shirt pocket where he usually keeps a pack of cigarettes, but it is empty. Just as well he's quit again, she thinks, or she would have to be inhospitable and remind him to smoke outside. "You know Adam Warner?" he goes on. "He used to live in town there? His ex is still here, eh. He went up to Wollaston Lake five years ago to teach a course in small motor mechanics and ended up going native, settling onto the reserve with an Indian girl."

She gives him a mock sour look.

"Then there was Martin Semchuck, went up to Fond du Lac to go fishing one summer and just disappeared. Twenty-five years ago, and no one's seen him since."

"Yes, I've heard about that. He drowned. It's no mystery, they just couldn't find the body in that big lake." She pours coffee and asks about Marjorie and the kids.

"Oh, they're all fine. Twins starting high school next year, can you believe it?"

No, she can't. They chat about time passing until he makes another futile pass at his shirt pocket and asks, "So are you doing okay?" By his abrupt, rather uncomfortable look of concern she can tell he is here because Marjorie told him to check up on her while he had the chance. "I'm heading into town and then on to P.A. I could get your mail, pick up some groceries for you," he offers.

"I'm fine," she says. Then the grocery list catches her eye, stuck to the fridge with a magnet, a souvenir of Dresden shaped like a ladybug. How nice it would be to have them all delivered. She could write him a cheque. "Well actually, I haven't been feeling that great lately. Sort of flu-ish."

"Give me a list, then, and I'll drop off your stuff on my way home," he says, as she knew he would.

··

AFTER ROBBIE DROPS off her groceries, she is afraid he'll tell Marjorie to look in on her again. Lisa looked like hell, he'd say, which if anything would give Marjorie a lift.

Soon after Lisa and Gerhardt moved out to the acreage, Robbie started coming over for coffee when she was alone in the afternoons. After one particularly friendly visit, she realized with tired dismay he was interested in her. She'd thought until then that the pointed glances, casual but questioning, were simple curiosity. But after he made her laugh as he was getting up to leave, he touched her arm just below the shoulder, the touch lingering a bit too long before he walked out the door. Next time he came over, she stonewalled him, acted brusque and hurried. She told funny stories about Gerhardt's Red Green home repairs, about his plans for their next holiday. She wondered if Robbie needed help with the haying; she would ask Gerhardt about it. Robbie's visits petered out.

The last time Marjorie and Robbie were over for drinks, Marjorie had too many rye and 7s and made a comment about her husband thinking he was still King of Stud City. "But he should take a good look at himself in the mirror," she said.

"*Mayor* of Stud City," Robbie had corrected, grinning evenly. That was over five years ago, Lisa realizes.

Now Robbie drops in to talk to Gerhardt about the cattle he and Lisa let graze on their bit of pasture. Gerhardt has coffee over there when he lends or borrows tools. Lisa and Marjorie hardly ever see each other on purpose. When Lisa runs into her and Robbie in town, she sometimes senses vague but complicated vibrations. She thinks it isn't so much Robbie's flirting with her that Marjorie resents, but that she rejected him outright.

King of Stud *Island*, Marjorie could have said. She knows, especially now that she has asked Robbie for help, that Marjorie might feel obliged to visit her again. What she should do is make a pre-emptive strike: wash and blow-dry her hair, put on makeup and decent clothes, and take a walk over to the Danielsons'. Assure them she is perfectly fine, so they can return to neighbourly indifference.

In earlier days, before she and Lisa realized they weren't destined to be friends, Marjorie would come over fairly often for a drink or coffee, and one afternoon she told her about Robbie's disastrous emu project. Hoping to make a fortune in the late eighties, he'd bought two mating pairs, talked into it one booze-filled night outside of P.A. in a friend's hot tub. There never had been a market, Marjorie said, only sales of horrendously expensive breeding pairs to people wanting to get in on the next big thing. It wouldn't have been so bad if the feed hadn't cost so much. Years later and thousands of dollars in the hole, Robbie had called another friend, a butcher, to come and help him with the slaughter.

Lisa was appalled. "Fifty birds? You're kidding."

"Thirty of them were still too small to butcher for meat, but the rest... Well, we supplied ourselves and everybody we knew. It's lean, very good really. Perfect for anyone who won't eat beef. The hamburger, you almost can't tell the difference." She got up from

Lisa's kitchen table and poured herself another drink. "Robbie was just sick for quite a while afterwards. He said it was the worst day of his life."

"Yes. I can imagine."

"No, you can't." Marjorie's chin sharpened with distaste. "Robbie and Marv are both good shots, but emus have such pea brains, shooting them in the head didn't always do the job. Some of the birds they shot even at close range would keep running around in a panic. It was unbelievable. They finally... Aw, shit." She sat down and took a long drink. "Let's talk about something else."

"What? What did they do!?"

"You don't want to know." Marjorie clammed up.

Two small emus escaped, and when they were rounded up, Robbie said fuck it, they'd just keep them. "As pets, sort of," Marjorie said grimly. "As reminders, I keep telling him."

Lisa knows better than to ask Robbie about it.

She digs into the groceries, putting away chicken and steak, fresh fruit and vegetables, milk and cheese, filling up the sparkling whiteness inside her fridge. How nice of him to do this for her. She would make a Greek salad and chicken breast and mashed potatoes. Damn. She should have thought to ask him to stop at the liquor store.

··

THAT NIGHT she dreams again, but this time she is doing the shooting, at something or someone. In the morning, all she can recall is the heft of a rifle in her hands, the excitement of aiming through crosshairs. Her uncle Max taught her to shoot a .22 up north at the cabin. She practised shooting a tin can off a stump until she became pretty good at it. She shot a sparrow once and will never forget the drop of blood on his beak, the neat hole through his chest, the absolute inertness of a death that was her fault.

What crime could Ben Meisner have committed that was so unspeakable he lied about it, sitting across from her at his kitchen table, his face heavy with pain, his eyes magnified by images of remembered horror? She remembers a quote from Primo Levi's *Survival in Auschwitz* and finds it again:

> *Just as our hunger is not that feeling of missing a meal, so our way of being cold has need of a new word. We say "hunger," we say "tiredness," "fear," "pain," we say "winter" and they are different things. They are free words, created and used by free men who lived in comfort and suffering in their own homes.*

She should tell Mr. Meisner she isn't the person he needs to talk to, that he should see somebody, a therapist, a rabbi. But she is the one who asked him for his story.

She grabs carpet shampoo from the porch cupboard and goes to work on the area rugs in the living room. She creates a satisfyingly greyish cloud of foam using a sponge, a scrub brush, and, as Aunt Gemma would say, elbow grease. She empties all the bookcases, brushes and dusts each book, polishes the wooden shelves to a glossy finish.

She finds the book Mr. Meisner lent her, *The Tunnel*. Paging through it, she reads a section that he'd marked with pencil.

> *Lay the length of a lasting love alongside any hate, that of the Armenians, for instance, the Turks for the Greeks, the Serbs for everybody. Do you suppose if the Armenians had been done a good turn back then, instead of being thinned,*

they would remember? Three square meals and clean clothes
in corded bales and darned blankets and bandages and
modern medicines for their festers and their flu? Would such
deeds be held tenderly against generations of grateful hearts?
No one would think so. No one. No.

But Ben Meisner doesn't seem to her to be full of hate for anyone.

THIRTEEN

Suzanne emails about her mother's poor health, her father's senility. Lisa answers, sympathizing, recounts more stories about Gerhardt, Man of the North, from his evening phone calls. She doesn't say anything about her own preoccupations. She can't bring herself to see any of it written down.

She is pleased to see a long email from Tyler. They decided they wanted to go somewhere they had friends, where they felt at home, so they returned to Bulgaria. He goes on at some length about their friends, Marco and Tatyana. Wanting to practise their English, they'd offered him and Céline a room, very cheap, for a couple of months. They decided to take them up on it as Céline hadn't been feeling well lately—she felt nauseous off and on and needed a rest from travelling. Lisa writes him an amused account of his dad's living conditions, although she knows Gerhardt emails Tyler himself. She copies the text and sends it on to Stephanie, even though she never checks her email. What communicating she does is with friends on MSN or over her cell phone, when she can pay the fees.

She tells Tyler that if Céline feels ill, can't they afford to see a doctor there, and if not, she could wire them some money. Wire. Is that still the right word? Of course Céline would ask her own parents for money if she needed any. Lisa just hopes she isn't pregnant. "At the doctor's," she writes, "make sure she takes her friend with her to translate." But all she can feel is dim concern, as if she were a distant entity looking down on someone else's life. She dials the Caribou Point School office number, then hangs up before it rings. She forwards Tyler's message instead. Céline likely just has some travel bug.

She's seen Tyler and Céline together only a few times, but she has to admit they seem to be in love. Touching each other. Looks passed over the dining table. Each with a slightly lost expression when the other isn't there. So she should get used to Céline. Gerhardt accepted her right from the start with the rather amused, or maybe bemused, geniality he shows to all Tyler's girlfriends.

She hopes they really are doing all right. Sometimes Tyler keeps his troubles to himself, doesn't want to worry his parents when they have so much to put up with from his sister. Even when he was little, he seemed to feel the need to entertain them. What was that Swedish movie? *My Life as a Dog*, where the boy recalls his dead mother in the same scene over and over, the two of them on the beach with him acting the clown, her laughing. It is so exactly what a boy would choose to remember fondly: making his mother laugh. She feels the pocket of her jeans, needing a Kleenex at the mere thought of it. Ach. She is fed up with herself always crying at movies. The death of Old Yeller. Ingrid Bergman walking away into the fog with her dorky husband. *Sophie's Choice*. Oh Christ, she would make herself sick.

She googles herself. Other Lisa Brauns' family trees, Facebook, and business web pages. One reference actually to her, left over on a Department of Education site from years ago when she'd worked with Suzanne on a curriculum guide in Saskatoon. Farther down, websites on Eva Braun. Not for the first time, she wonders if there might be a distant connection to Gerhardt's family, and regrets not keeping her maiden name.

..

WHILE REREADING Hannah Arendt, she writes Tyler another email. "I've been thinking about when you and Stephanie were teenagers and read those books on the Holocaust." Although it was Stephanie who'd done most of the reading, she has decided to recall him doing so as well. "Do you remember Hannah Arendt's chapter on Bulgaria, about how the people there refused to betray their Jewish citizens? Why do you think that was? Have you seen anything in the Bulgarian character that might explain this? The Danes, too, resisted. I wonder if you've noticed any similarities? I've been thinking about such things lately, and maybe am alone too much since Dad and Suzanne have been gone. At any rate, I want to know your opinion."

The phone rings again. This time it is a school and she doesn't answer. They don't have voicemail. With call display, Gerhardt doesn't think it necessary since he has a message manager at work, and now she is glad not to have it. The fewer voices she has to deal with the better. She gets up and makes coffee.

She hasn't answered the phone to any schools since the high school social studies class. Marjorie has a relative working in the P.A. school board office, and Lisa has begun to worry she'll tell Marjorie that she hasn't been working at all. Not that she cares about them gossiping, as long as Marjorie doesn't decide to make her one of her pet projects, or even worse, to sic church ladies from town on her. Even without her neighbour's interference, she is a sitting duck for Jehovah's Witnesses, not to mention any do-gooders from the Lutherans or Uniteds. But what is she thinking?

Sunshine Sketches of a Little Town? This isn't 1912. People in Cullen might gossip, but they mind their own business. She isn't part of the community; she's been here only eight years and hasn't made an effort. Never joined a curling team or attended local hockey games, didn't volunteer at the kindergarten or the seniors' lodge. Until now.

With her bag of rags and a bucket of soapy water, she washes the car, rinses it with the garden hose, waxes and polishes until she sees her reflection in a new-car sheen. The sky is cloudless, but she decides to park the gleaming Toyota in the garage. It has been so long since she needed her keys, she doesn't know where they are. At the bottom of her purse, of course. Then the overhead door won't open. Dead batteries in the remote control. She adjusts the door to manual and heaves it open herself. She should take the car for a spin to charge up the battery, she thinks, but drives into the garage.

··

BY THE TIME Ben Meisner phones, wild rosebuds are flushing pink along her walking trail and, except for the walls, she has cleaned the house all over again. "I intended to call earlier," he says.

"I wasn't going anywhere," she says.

FOURTEEN

"The truth now. In 1939 I reached home crazed with horror, with as they now say so benignly, post-traumatic stress disorder. Disorder. You've read Mann's *Disorder and Early Sorrow*? He couldn't fathom what early sorrow some children just like his characters would endure in the coming years. Children! But yes. After some weeks of rest, eating healthy food, I was able to gather strength, but then my mother's care caused a reaction. I became possessed, taken over by nightmare visions of what would be done to my gentle parents.

"I cannot say even now that what I did wasn't for the best. But I have not had a whole peaceful hour since. All my blessings are like apples with a spot of rot I can never cut out. You may say that Buchenwald would have spoiled my life no matter what happened to my parents, but that is beside the point.

"I have talked about their fate to no one, and I want your word that you won't tell. I would not want my son or daughter to know of this. There was a time I could have told my wife, but that time came and went and I took no advantage of it. We lived virtually separate lives toward the end, and when she died, I was there, but she died alone. As does everyone. There is a book called *Every*

Man Dies Alone. I have few books anymore; for the little I read now, I use the library. That novel is by a German, and shows how it was then for the ordinary citizen. The fear that seeped like putrid garbage through everything. It doesn't justify Buchenwald, but it makes one to understand some things. Fear incapacitates, causes a form of quadriplegia. I think of those people on the bus. No one looking at me. I know they believed what I said.

"All this truth and reconciliation in Africa, or in the residential schools here. I don't know what goes on in other victims' minds. Who can forgive torture, butchery? But I can at least theoretically forgive some of the ordinary Germans' cowardice, our neighbours turning their backs because of fear. That I can understand: fear.

"Perhaps the average citizen truly did not have any idea. That is of course what they say. The Americans, when they liberated Buchenwald, made the townspeople take a tour of the camp. They reported that the mayor and his wife then committed suicide, and the Americans seemed to think this was a positive sign, that the ordinary German really hadn't known and was deathly ashamed, as appalled by Buchenwald as the rest of the world. But I think they killed themselves from the shame of being caught out. I would bet my life, paltry as it is now, that those two were sickened not by the facts of the camp, with which they were already familiar, but by the prospect of how the world would now regard them.

"In my own defence, if my mother and father had fully understood and believed what was before them, truly comprehended the stories I told of the camp, they would indeed have killed themselves. But they held on to hope. People always cling to hope, which is why it was one of Pandora's evils. I believe, along with Nietzsche, that hope is the worst evil of them all.

"We lived near a high, narrow bridge over the Weser River, never much traffic, that I used to seek out as a refuge. When I was a student, at night I would walk to the bridge and stand looking at the water, at the reflecting lights, and reflect myself, yes, on my adolescent concerns and dreams, on philosophical conundrums. My mother would admonish me for being a night owl, thought I was out meeting a girl.

"After weeks of convalescence, I was feeling stronger. I was at the window of my room watching the bridge, although all I could see was an outline. I couldn't sleep, not only for fear of nightmares, but fear that my being at home was a dream, that I would wake up and find myself back in the camp. I could not clear my mind and was obsessed, overpowered by fear for my parents.

"Picture this: Picture your own mother and father at any time of their lives, or no, think of yourself at eighteen, nineteen, think of the age they were then, and then picture them tortured in the ways you've read or heard me talk about. Beaten, starved, forced to stand for hours, cudgelled, whipped, worse. You can't picture it, I know. Images such as those escape, won't come to you. But they came to me because I'd seen them, seen them happen to others older than my parents. Experienced them. They would have suffered in cattle cars, been tortured and starved, and would have been gassed. I could not get the sight of fellow Jews—what they did to them, what they did to me—out of my mind.

"I knew, knew without a doubt that my mother and father would be sent to a camp. I knew there were other camps like Buchenwald. I knew then what few other people, even Jews, would believe at the time, and I could not bear it. I had to end that fear, and one night I left the house, drawn to the bridge. Once there, I climbed the railing where there was a temporary platform on one section, for workmen changing lights I suppose. I stood there and thought, one little movement and the horror of my existence would be gone. But what good would this do my mother, my father, who would still have to endure the camps? And have to endure my suicide besides? I stood and thought.

"Then out of nowhere they were there, my parents. They had come looking, had risked being out at night, although nobody was patrolling the area then. On that night there was no one about at all.

"They cried my name, climbed onto the platform, grabbed my arms, and I had...it was a brainstorm. I calmed, calmed right down, talked to them, and began my descent. I was one step below them now. I gathered my strength, and then broke. In a storm of rage at this life, I gave a shove from that step below, shoved my mother against my father. I had the advantage of shock and the strength of the insane, and they fell. Neither could swim.

"I stood for I don't know how long watching the black depths for a sign, and saw nothing. I walked home in a trance. Saved. It seemed a miracle to me. Drowning in deep or breaking their necks in shallow water, I never knew. Better than months of starvation and torture before having their heads smashed in or forced to breathe poison. That is what I thought then, and yes, what I think now. But the horror of having done it! I was insane. I had been driven mad. I will never forgive. Not only the Nazis but myself.

"I should have jumped then, committed suicide. That would have been...apt. But I made my way home, slept strangely peacefully the rest of the night. I woke up afraid that the police would soon be there after finding the bodies. I hid all day in the coal cellar, which was cleared out in summer, and then that night, I made my escape.

"Yes, after nights of walking, I came to that garden in a beech forest where I was able to find refuge. Ach, it was not only beech trees. There were scrub oaks too, and bushes, some with fruit, berries. I made a slingshot with rubber from an old bike inner tube I'd found along the way and shot partridge, and managed to snare rabbits with wire from the shed. A city boy, I was lucky to know how. I had a friend, Werner, who when we were young teenagers was in a scout group, something of a predecessor of Hitler Youth. Yes, I did have that one friend, I was mistaken to say I had no one. He lived in a nearby apartment block, and for some time his parents quietly allowed us to visit each other. Werner learned to set up camp in the woods, set traps, and tie various knots, and he taught me what he'd learned, and we imagined how we would survive if lost in a wilderness. But soon enough he was forbidden to see me. Or he just quit on his own. I heard later he died in the war.

"The shed also held a book I'd left behind from my studies a few years earlier, and I was thankful for it. No, not Nietzsche, Schopenhauer. He with his pessimistic comfort. The book and the wire were the only things that hadn't been looted besides a couple of large tin cans I used for cooking along with my light frying pan. All the blankets were gone, the sleeping mats, lamps, utensils, but I made a bed with dry moss and my coat. I'd brought along candles, matches, the frying pan, army knife, that sort of thing. There was a spring nearby that had good water. After weeding the garden, I found a few carrots and onions that had survived or reseeded, and sprouting potatoes. New asparagus grew quickly after I cut it down. I could recognize a couple of types of edible mushrooms in the forest. Asparagus with mushrooms, a feast you can't imagine.

"People from the nearest hamlet had never been interested in going out there—it was too far for a comfortable walk—but I was always afraid somebody might show up. The place had already been looted. I was sure someone would eventually recall the existence of a shack and garden and look in, for curiosity's sake, on a hike, or maybe to take them over. There was a small stove. I tried to cook only at night to keep the smoke invisible. I thought if I found it impossible to cross the Danish border, maybe I could return and try to last the winter there.

"The longer I was there, the more anguish I endured from guilt. I kept telling myself I'd been deranged, that a lunatic committed that crime. I still do that. Tell myself. The beech trees, the grey smoothness of their bark—I used to rub my hands over a certain tree trunk near the hut and derive comfort as if it were an animal. I walked long distances through the woods, once or twice having to hide from voices in the distance, people who had likely come to pick berries or mushrooms. I developed such dread of being seen that it became a phobia. My hope was to become invisible, to develop a form of non-existence until I was out of Germany. I sometimes to this day think I managed to do just that.

"So. My story is now finished. I am a murderer of the worst kind. I excuse myself, I tell myself I was crazy, I did it out of love, prevented my mother and father from suffering, et cetera. But in the end, I know it was a selfish act. Because of it, I was able to leave, to survive."

FIFTEEN

On a website called *Philosophy for Dummies*, Lisa finds a quote from Schopenhauer. It describes tragedy as the highest poetic art because it accurately portrays human life: "...the unspeakable pain, the wail of humanity, the triumph of evil, the mocking mastery of chance and the irretrievable fall of the just and innocent."

Why had he chosen to tell her after already lying, saying his parents' deaths had been suicide? She can't recall any change in his attitude last time, no sudden realization that she might be someone out of the ordinary.

In spite of what he said in the end, she is supposed to think of this murder as a mercy killing. But he could have left his parents, taken off for the border alone, with the hope they would survive. Of course, then he would have been ravaged by worry. He loved them, was maybe too close to them, and allowed this to govern his actions. But wouldn't she too—wouldn't anyone in the same situation—want her parents dead rather than to suffer torture, to go through hell in a death camp, only to die anyway? And his justification to himself that he was insane was true. It wasn't premeditated; he'd been overwhelmed by a blind need for certainty.

She would need time to consider all that he'd had to overcome in order to live. She would recall it all in small doses when she felt free to think, to conjure his voice, the steady pitch, the way he sat there within his own atmosphere of crippled calm.

She wakes up in the middle of the night to the nagging surety she's forgotten something, something that needs to be done. The anxiety of wondering what it could be keeps her awake until she narrows it down to cleaning. The ceiling lights. All that dust inside them, the desiccated flies and legs of spiders. How could she not have done them while she was washing the ceiling? Images of each light click through her mind like slides in an old projector, until with the dawn at 4 a.m., she gets up and fills the kitchen sink with hot soapy water. Standing on a chair, she removes the light shades in every room (how could she not have done this already?), carefully storing the screws in separate egg cups. She washes each milky glass globe, each leaf-patterned curved plate, each disc from the hanging lamp in the dining room, rinses and polishes, then puts them all back. Eventually, she goes to bed and sleeps.

..

SHE DRIFTS IN and out of consciousness, listening to the phone ring as if it were a distant train whistle. Cocooned in the silky cotton of the six-hundred-thread-count sheets she bought at Winners, she means to answer but sinks back into the arms of Morpheus. Morphine. Opium. Heroin. She wonders what it would be like to give yourself over to a drug, just give up altogether. It would be lovely. But an image of Stephanie, nodding in a corner of the living room, catches her off guard: no it wouldn't. Before she falls back to sleep, she checks to see who's been phoning. Oh, Gerhardt. Who else?

It is late afternoon before the phone rings again. It's Gerhardt's cell phone this time, so he must be somewhere he can access a signal. She sits up straight so her voice won't sound as if she's been sleeping. "Hello?"

"Lisa. I tried to call you earlier."

"Oh yes, well, I've been outside."

"I'm here in P.A."

"What!?"

"I'm at the airport, I just got in. Can you pick me up?"

"My god. You're here?"

"Yes. I'm taking a taxi to the office, and you can pick me up there. I'll order some Chinese food so we can eat supper when you get in." He pauses. "Are you okay?"

"Um, yes. I'm fine. But what are you doing here?" Has he been fired? Quit? Has some final straw in his living conditions pissed him off?

"I just need a break, so I'm taking a long weekend."

Rinsing her face and brushing her teeth give her some energy, but seeing the state of her hair almost sets her back. She can't allow herself time to take a shower, so she washes her armpits and finds a decent T-shirt. She ties her hair back, dons silver earrings, puts on lipstick, and heads out the door in the jeans she found pooled beside the bed.

Once on the highway, she relaxes enough to set the cruise control at a respectable speed and coasts. The sun slants off newly headed crops and roadside grasses, turning green to gold. It must already be early evening. She forgot her watch and the car's digital clock is no help, flashing its perpetual midnight, or noon.

Downtown Prince Albert is deserted at this time of day. Gerhardt's office, a small room on the first floor of an old three-storey block, is just off Central Avenue. For once she is able to park in front of the building. The slanted rays of the sun which beautified the scenery out of town now highlight the coarse dust sifting over cement and brick, the potato chip and grocery bags blowing past grimy plate-glass windows and their tired displays of spring jackets, running shoes, bargain furniture.

Before she can get her key in the lock, Gerhardt opens the door. He's been watching for her. They say hello, hug and kiss briefly before he stands back to let her in. She feels an unaccountable sense of carefulness. Trying to displace it, she pinches his midriff. "You're getting fat," she says.

He grins. "I can't go jogging up there. Too many dogs."

She can smell food from WK Kitchen. She holds him for a moment, grateful as usual for his broad chest and sheltering shoulders.

"So," he says, "did you miss me?"

Abruptly, she sinks into the irritation and comfort of her marriage and feels as if she is the one who just got home. "Let's eat," she says.

··

HE DOESN'T NOTICE how clean the house is until she points it out the next morning. Then he walks through the spotless rooms, admiring just to be polite, she thinks. But later, happening to glance upwards from his lunch in the kitchen, he stands abruptly and cranes his neck. "You didn't wash the *ceiling*, did you?"

"Yes. And all the walls."

He sits down again, takes a sip of coffee, his forehead furrowed as if she were causing fragments of him to age instantaneously. "Lisa, are you all right?" Realizing that being worried about a clean house is ridiculous, he glances up at the ceiling again, shakes his head, and grins.

They didn't talk much last night. Over supper they discussed the kids, comparing notes on Stephanie's sparse communications and what Tyler and Céline could possibly find so interesting in Bulgaria. After driving home, there was sex to manage, which went well all things considered, and then she fell into a surprisingly heavy sleep, interrupted once or twice by him getting out of bed, prowling the house in the dark.

"I'm fine. Or at least, I'm doing okay. I've been..." Why not just tell him everything? She tells him as simply as she can what getting to know Ben Meisner had started: his story, the history class, and her internet research. She leaves out his final confession. As she talks, Gerhardt's eyes acquire their cold greyish cast.

They leave the kitchen table for the living room, where he sits on the couch, his face set, his hands pressed together. "I don't understand why this has now come up after all these years. I mean, I suppose I can understand wanting to listen to his memories, but doing more research is so self-defeating. Masochistic almost."

"I don't know," she says, looking past him at their print of a Group of Seven tree growing out of a rock. "Maybe it's just that I'm not used to so much time alone. And after getting to know Ben Meisner, I just... I felt I needed to know more."

"It's too bad Suzanne had to leave," he says, "right at the same time as me."

The phone rings, and he reaches for the cordless. "Hello?"

It's likely Marjorie, phoning on some pretense or other. She must have seen the car come and go past her house.

"What? Who is this?" He listens impatiently. "I don't answer surveys. No. You've got the wrong number." He hangs up. "Statistics Canada," he says, disgusted. "Wasting people's time."

She bends her head, rubbing her eyes. Another month has passed.

∙∙

THE FEW TIMES they talked about the Holocaust in the past, its emotional significance made them awkward, overpowered anything they had to say. It was only able to be discussed at a certain personal level. Years ago, Gerhardt told her about seeing a film on the death camps when it had toured Germany in the sixties. He described nothing of what he saw, but he'd left the theatre to be sick, and had gone through his own depression after that and come through it. He'd been a teenager then. She knows he isn't about to join her in crisis now, all these years later. He doesn't say this aloud, but for the remainder of the weekend they return to their usual way of being with each other, shadowed by an undertone that would probably go away in time if she could just get herself together.

"I think I'll try to get out more," she says. "I'm sort of taking a break from teaching, but I might start doing a few more things at Pioneer Lodge." They are walking together down the old Métis trail. He is to leave in an hour to go back north. "Maybe I can carpool with Marjorie," she lies. The bush on either side is overgrown, with wild roses in full bloom, chokecherries forming hard new berries. The aspens with their misshapen branches stand a poisonous green against the sparsely branched pines and near black of spruce trees.

She thinks that he'll object, that he'll worry about her continuing to see Mr. Meisner, but he doesn't say anything. He retains something of a shell-shocked look, his eyes not entirely rid of their grey lustre. She can tell he is anxious to return to work.

After he's gone, she phones Statistics Canada and tells them from now on they should wait until she calls them.

··

SHE ISN'T SURE Ben Meisner will want to see her again, but she wants him to think well of her and not to regret his decision to tell the truth. She has to let him know she isn't repelled by his story. She lets a couple of days pass and drives into Cullen. She doesn't know what will happen now. They could become better friends. They might never see each other again. She could visit him a few more times and drift away.

On his front step, she is struck this time by colour; his small front garden plot is blooming in a spectacular display of irises and yellow lilies, much superior to those in her own garden.

"You have such beautiful flowers!" she says, a bit too enthusiastically.

"I plan for a continuous show," he says, inviting her in. "After these are done, the lady's mantle takes over, and I plant annuals. Maybe petunias. Or perhaps lavatera. They are spectacular, but pink. Not so appropriate for a man's front garden, eh?"

"If you wanted a display of machismo you wouldn't grow any flowers at all."

This time he leads her past the kitchen into the living room to the small couch, and he sits on a checked monstrosity, a combination rocking and easy chair. He offers her coffee and Peek Freans, but he is not about to make polite conversation. "I hope you have taken to heart what I requested," he says.

What did he request? After a moment's unease, she asks, "You mean not to tell anyone? Of course I won't."

"Especially my daughter. She visits every few weeks. I don't want her to worm anything out of you if she finds out you've been seeing me." He eats a cookie as if he were referring to nothing more important than local gossip. "She'll wonder what we've been talking about."

"She shouldn't find it too odd. It was part of my job as a volunteer to help you with the garden, and to visit people, for that matter. Why wouldn't I see you again once I've got to know you?"

"Yes. But who else have you visited? Why are you interested in me? Because you are married to a German, you might want to know my story. For whatever reason." He eyes her keenly. "Simone might wonder if I've told you anything." He pronounces his daughter's name in the German way, with three syllables: *See-mo-neh.*

In a sudden distracted silence, he leans back in his creaky chair and drinks his coffee. She catches a glimpse of him as a teenager, a philosophy student admiring lights on the water. "I think I told you that you were the only one to ever hear about Buchenwald?" he asks.

"Yes."

"Well then, I lied. I didn't want to bring her into this, but now I can't see why not. I told Simone's daughter, my granddaughter Kerry, when she was a teenager. I described some of what I went through. Not as much as I told you."

"Your daughter knows then. At least something about the camp, I mean. Kerry would have told her."

"Kerry would have told her nothing. They weren't close then and they're not now." He looks at the floor in silence. "When Kerry was seventeen, she tried to starve herself." He says this harshly. Disgusted. "My flesh and blood, after all I'd gone through, on purpose looking as if she were someone who'd been through the camps. I went to see her in the hospital to tell her something of Buchenwald. Of the hunger. I said she was making a mockery."

"How is she now?"

"She decided to live. I don't think it had anything to do with my talk with her. But she is now obese. Morbid. Again, as if she is mocking me. Pah. She was such a lovely girl."

Lisa thinks about her own daughter as a teenager, reading Hannah Arendt, but remains silent, helping him eat all the cookies. She likes Peek Freans, hasn't thought to buy them in years.

She asks if he has read Arendt. "She said only the Danes and the Bulgarians had the strength of character to refuse to turn their Jewish citizens over to the Nazis. Why do you think that was? Do you have any idea from dealing with the Danes?"

"The Danes. Yes, I will always be grateful to them."

"Do you think there's something in their national character? Or was it their circumstances?"

He ponders the empty cookie plate. "I suppose it was a combination of the two. Their Jews had always lived there as ordinary citizens. But for some time, so had we in Germany. As far as I can recall, in day-to-day life the Danes seemed no better or worse than anyone else. The Swedes too, although they harboured all of us who escaped." He seems preoccupied, not too interested in the inscrutability of the Scandinavians.

"I can understand you not wanting your daughter to know about your parents, but why don't you want her to know what happened to you in the camp?"

"I don't want to burden my children with bitterness. If I tell them about my experiences, they won't be able to help imagining me, to try to fathom me undergoing...and blaming, preoccupied with the people who could do those things to me, to their father. Would you want to know horrors like that about your father? And to wonder where his torturers are now, not to mention what he was capable of doing then in order to survive? They know enough already. Everyone does."

She considers, pictures her dad as he was in middle age, his bald head shining in the sun as he mowed the lawn. "Maybe not when I was young. I might not want such traumatic knowledge to affect my whole life. But now, at my age, I think I would like to know. My life at this point is the way it is, nothing much can tilt it one way or the other." She wonders if that is a lie.

"It is for me," he points to his chest. "I would rather she not know." He gives her a covert look. She notices again how his eyes are slightly magnified by his glasses. "I'm glad you dropped by. I was going to give you a call. I want to ask you a favour."

She nods and sips her cooling coffee. He made an atrocious brew, like typical small-town café dishwater left to gather strength by sitting too long. "Sure," she says.

"Simone lives in Regina. Benjamin, my son, in Toronto. Both of them were out here two summers ago insisting I give up my car, give up driving. I was not happy." He glares resentfully at Lisa, as if she were his daughter. She tries to look sympathetic. "They bullied me into it. In the end, I sold the car for their peace of mind, but I still have my licence. So. I want to borrow your car one day to drive out to my old farm site." He nods as if assuring himself of something. "The house is falling in, but the garage is in quite good shape. The people who bought the land have shown no signs of moving it away." He rises ponderously to pour himself another cup. "I wish to spend an entire day there, alone."

She knows his family must have made him give up his car for a reason. She glances again at his glasses, hasn't really thought before what their thickness means. "You're sure you're okay to drive?" She can't turn over her car to someone who can't see, no matter how much she wants to help him out.

"Oh yes. In any case, I could make my way out to the farm blindfolded." Seeing he has struck the point of her main worry, he flashes her a sly look and grins.

This is the first time since his story that she's seen him really smile. So this is how it is. It's possible to be amused, to exist minute by minute and just live life in spite of everything. "Oh, why not?" she says. "Of course you can borrow my car. I'll come over whatever day you like and you can drop me off at home." That way she'd know if he could drive or not. "Then when you leave the farm, come straight to my place and I'll give you a lift back here."

"Thank you. I will call you next week."

··

WHEN A WEEK went by and he didn't call, she was relieved. She could understand him wanting to spend some time out at his old homestead. Maybe this would be his last opportunity to see it again. But she should have offered to drive him herself, not to be there with him, but to come back for him at a set time. She pours herself a glass of wine and wanders through the house, wondering if she should give him a call and suggest that. But she has promised the use of her car. Maybe he's had second thoughts and will forget the whole idea. At any rate, she feels she owes him something.

She will do what she can for him, which isn't much. He's already living in a place that monitors his wellbeing, and he is in reasonable health for someone in his mid-eighties. He will need transportation to places he wants to go. Picturing him at his kitchen table, she is struck by his resemblance to someone familiar. His build is similar to Gerhardt's; maybe when he was younger, he and her husband had the same kind of physical presence. And that air of German single-mindedness, a stubborn refusal to compromise.

She continues to drift through her house, admiring the long green view down to the creek from the living room, stopping by the kitchen window to contemplate her garden. Her creation. Mr. Meisner could visit her this summer, give her advice on how to grow healthier delphiniums. He could shoot the breeze with Gerhardt in German, and she could improve her language skills. But no.

She is surrounded by light and beauty, beauty out of every window. The late afternoon sunshine has an odd orange cast to it, as if the light were partly synthesized, the garden being filmed for a surreal movie. She should start painting again, do a series of window views like the piece she displays in her living room. That would be derivative, of course—it has been done before, now by a popular American whose prints you can buy at Sears. In fact, she thinks the artist's name is Brown. But so what? These would be for no one but herself.

She pours herself another glass and switches on the TV. She surfs channels, searching for a few mindless minutes with Oprah, but stops instead at Judge Judy.

The judge, hectoring, opinionated, with such self-confidence and sarcastic wit. True, there is no contest; her victims are generally poor white trash, or Black and Hispanic equivalents. Hangdog and inarticulate. And Judy so Jewish. What would happen if these sad-sack losers—that kid with the mullet she just called a bozo on national television—what if he were granted the ability to hunt her down, to turn her in, to guard her in a camp? Oh, Judge Judy, be careful, watch out, you'd be one of the first to go.

She turns off the TV and instead gazes at the light outside, the sun still casting its weird brightness over the garden. Like the light in Mazatlán, on a trip there once with Gerhardt, the Mexican sun hazing through white curtains that ballooned in the warm breeze against white bedroom walls. Lust enhanced somehow by all the light and the white into a delicious torment.

She has always been an afternoon person. So many white afternoons with Gerhardt in warm countries. She puts her wine glass carefully on the coffee table, undoes her jeans, and lies down on the couch, but gets up unsatisfied. She needs a penis, a body, real sex. God. How old is she? Take a cold shower, get some exercise. Gerhardt will be home soon, and she hopes she can reincarnate this horniness when he can appreciate it.

The phone rings. It is Ben Meisner, wondering if he can borrow her car in the morning. He'll be ready, he says, for 8:30. She mentions her idea of driving him herself. "No." He is definite. "I need to drive there on my own."

Outside, walking in her garden, she realizes the strange light is caused by traces of smoke from a forest fire. A holocaust in the old sense of the word, a thousand miles away.

SIXTEEN

She tells herself he wouldn't have a licence if he weren't able to drive, that a doctor would have made sure it was taken away. Then again, she hasn't actually seen any documents from his wallet, and how would she have asked? Who was she to say "Show me your driver's licence" after all he'd told her? But if he hurt himself in an accident she'd never forgive herself. Trying to sleep, she pictures him driving her car into another vehicle or into the ditch, flipping over into a slough. Her mind circles the same images between night sweats and bouts of fitful slumber. The alarm rouses her into a stupefied daze.

She manages to get to Cullen only a few minutes late. Ben Meisner is waiting outside his door, holding a small backpack with what she assumes to be his lunch. She hears the clink of a bottle as, becoming momentarily agile, he slips quickly into the passenger side before she has a chance to get out. Shit. He knows damn well she wants to see what kind of driver he is.

Once, she thinks. She will do him this favour one time, and if he wants to go anywhere again, she'll drive him herself. He holds the backpack on his lap, intent, quiet, like a kid on his first day of school. Christ, is there really a bottle in there? He'll end up getting plastered and then trying to drive. "You know the way?" she asks, turning carefully onto the road out of town. "How to get from my place to your old farm and back again?" Maybe it's only beer.

"Oh certainly," he says. He keeps his face turned away, looking out the side window at the crops of budding canola, the silken brushes of barley. Once they are off the highway, he keeps his eyes on the grid road winding up in front of them like a spool of tan-coloured ribbon. When they reach her house, he relaxes. "You have a beautiful place here."

"Thank you. The shingles need replacing, but you can't really notice that from this angle." In fact, the house and yard through someone else's eyes seem straight out of *Better Homes and Gardens*, a graceful bungalow set off by cedar shrubs and new ferns unfurling at the foundation, windows gleaming, the log siding well preserved. In the garden, late tulips and early lilies bloom, forget-me-nots are fading but still form small drifts of sky against layers of green. White anemones wave, bleeding hearts display graceful arcs of pink, fine-leafed meadow rue is beginning to show its smoky feathers. She feels a ridiculous surge of pride.

She invites him in for coffee, knowing he'll refuse. As he drives off, she tries not to gawk at the way he handles the car. He seems capable enough. He stays on the right side of the road and holds it steady.

Late in the afternoon, after repeatedly dozing off over a book, she can't resist the temptation to nestle into the couch pillows for a nap. She would wake up before supper, or when he got there for his ride home. He said he'd be all day, hadn't specified a return time, but she knows he can't have more than a couple of sand-wiches with him.

She falls into an exhausted sleep, only jolting awake after dark. She sits up, fuzzy and disoriented until worry zeroes in. It is late, and he isn't here yet. She dials his number in case he's been to her place and she didn't hear the doorbell. As she listens to the phone ring, counting ten, eleven, twelve before hanging up, all her fears from the previous night resurface. He hasn't shown up, and the sun has set on any chance of her going after him. She doesn't know where the farm is, just the general neighbourhood, and driving Gerhardt's old work van on these back roads at night would be like trying to fly without navigation. Has he fallen asleep out there? She feels sick with the knowledge that this would be the best of all possibilities. She should have asked outright if he had booze with him in his bag.

If he has had an accident and it's serious, the police would contact the owner of the car. Unless of course no one has found him yet. If it were only a fender bender, he'd have driven home and phoned her himself, or been here by now. Or maybe he is just waiting in a ditch for someone to show up and pull him out.

She has two choices: phone Robbie and Marjorie, or phone the cops. Robbie would be able to drive right out there; he knows every corner of the countryside around Cullen. So do the RCMP, from trolling the old farmsteads for parties of drunken teenagers. But what if he went in the ditch after driving drunk? Does she really want to send the cops after him? She dials the Danielsons' number.

"I'll come and pick you up," Robbie says. "If he's sick or confused, it would be better if you're along."

"Well of course, I didn't mean to send you out there on your own." Did she? "Is your cell phone charged up? Because mine might run out soon." She in fact doesn't know where hers is. She hasn't bought time on it since they came home from Germany. "Just in case we have to phone the Mounties." She didn't think to ask Mr. Meisner if he had a cell phone. As with the other elderly residents, his kids have probably given him one that he never uses.

Robbie's half-ton smells of axle grease and Old Spice. They don't say much on the drive along the back country roads. If this were Gerhardt driving, she'd tell him not to go so fast.

"What were you thinking anyways," Robbie finally says, "lending one of these old guys your car?"

What kind of tone is that? "I was volunteering; I took Marjorie's place while she was away, did some gardening with him. He just wanted to go out to his old place on his own, I didn't think anything of it. I've gotten to know him and he seems with it and capable enough." She doesn't mention the bottle. "Jeez," she says. "I should be watching the ditch."

"I've been doing that." Robbie nods toward the grass flashing by on her side. "Whatever the headlights can pick up."

"Maybe I should have just phoned the cops."

"Around here you only phone the cops for real emergencies. And even then…" He doesn't say what. "We're almost at Meisners' now. Look for a row of old spruce trees."

Although there's only a quarter-moon, the sky is bright enough with stars to reveal a black outline of rangy evergreens. Past them lies a farmstead sheltered by other old trees—elms, she realizes by their shape, hard to grow around here. A shaggy caragana hedge curves in a graceful arc around the house and garage, unlike the usual straight lines of most homesteads. As they jounce down the rough dirt driveway, the weathered two-storey house with its tin-sided garage flickers in the headlights as if in an old film. They stop. Her car isn't there.

Robbie turns off the ignition and they sit for some time, not sure where to go from here, the silence broken only by the pinging and tapping of the cooling motor. She hears her stomach rumble and realizes she hasn't had any supper.

The outline of an ancient rod weeder sits by the crumbled foundation of a demolished barn. At the edge of the property, an old granary leans against the indigo skyline.

"Look." Abruptly, Robbie points out a weak gleam through the garage window. Car lights, almost burnt out.

"What would he be sitting in there for? Parked in the garage." Then her stomach churns and she gasps weakly.

Robbie says, "Holy fuck."

Time slows to a hazy crawl as she watches him lope awkwardly toward the building. As she steps on the running board to follow him, her knees refuse to hold her up. She sits with the truck door open until she finds the strength to walk. By that time Robbie's high-powered flashlight has lit up the inside. As she nears the garage, he heaves the overhead door open. The car's lights are out now. "Robbie?" Hearing her voice come out high and shaky, she feels stupidly like Olive Oyl calling Popeye. Walking in, she glances into the car, where a dark form lies motionless on the back seat. Her breath stops as if she's taken a sudden plunge into cold water, but she makes a weak move toward the body. They have to check to see. "Don't," Robbie says. "I already felt for a pulse. He's dead."

Even with the garage doors open, the exhaust smell is overpowering. The gas tank was almost full. She touches Robbie's shoulder as he dials his cell phone. "Do that away from here," she says, "before you keel over yourself." She refuses to look again at the body and walks out. Ben Meisner isn't hers. Isn't her dad, her uncle. Just some acquaintance who has taken advantage of her.

Robbie directs the police to the farm site. After he hangs up, he says, "I'm not thinking straight. He sure felt dead to me, but I thought he still had some colour in his face. I should be calling an ambulance."

"The police will call an ambulance on their own. Besides, suppose the paramedics are able to save him. Would you feel good about that? He was old and ready to go." Her voice holds a peculiar spiteful undertone that she can't help.

Robbie won't look at her. "Maybe we should get the car out of there, air it out."

She takes a deep breath. She can't stop shaking, but most of it is with anger. Pure rage. "We shouldn't touch anything," she says. "It's the scene of a crime."

"It's suicide, not a crime."

It is a crime. Against his family. Against her. For doing him this one favour. "The car's out of gas, you couldn't move it anyway." He doesn't reply, but she knows if she volunteers to steer, he could push it out.

They sit on the rotting front steps of the house. The Milky Way sparkles above them, casting a net of such radiance she feels mocked, feels that the universe is telling her to lighten up, she is nothing but a meaningless atom anyway. A tiny particle of shit in the monumental lavatory of human existence.

"I need a smoke," Robbie says. "I don't suppose you have any?"

"I haven't smoked in years. But I wouldn't mind one now myself." She is still shaking, taking deep breaths to keep herself together. "What I'd really like is a drink," she says.

He looks at her sideways. "There's a bottle, still three-quarters full, in the car."

That is very good news. "You mean in the truck," she says.

"No. In your car."

Of course. The one Ben brought with him. But why would it be almost full?

"Rye. Next to an empty bottle of pills."

They sit gazing at the stars, pondering the possibilities. "Even if we had our own booze in the truck," she says, "we shouldn't drink anything with the cops coming. You have to drive."

"That's right." He rubs his chin. "Besides, they'll know he ingested alcohol if there's an autopsy, and they might wonder where the bottle went."

A contemplative silence takes over. She now feels as if a good part of her has been shot with novocaine. She holds her hand in front of her, as if blessing something, noting its newfound steadiness. But she still longs for a drink.

"We could pour some of it in a thermos I have in the glove compartment and drink it after they leave," Robbie suggests. "I need to check the body again anyway, just for my own peace of mind. I was sure he's dead, but…"

When Lisa doesn't answer, he searches his truck for the container and holds it up, its metal sides glowing a weak beacon in the starlight.

"Just don't leave any fingerprints," she calls.

In a minute or two he is back, tucking in the shirttail he'd used to protect the bottle. He looks grim. "There's no way he's alive." Almost immediately, his cell phone plays the chorus of "Like a Rock." "Jeez, the cops must be here already," he says. "Hello? Yeah, I'll turn my headlights on. Just east of a row of spruce there, can you see them?"

The ambulance they neglected to call arrives behind the police car. After examining the scene and watching the medics take Ben Meisner away, the lone Mountie sits making notes with his car door open. When he gets out to ask questions, Lisa expects to feel nervous, but the officer is only a boy, younger than Tyler. The way his ears stand out against the headlights brings on a brief nostalgia for summer nights, her young self or her children on visits to country relatives, playing kick the can under a yard light. She sees no reason to hide anything and tells him all she knows. Her volunteer work, her listening to Mr. Meisner's stories about Buchenwald. "I know dredging up those memories affected him. I was stupid to lend him the car." She starts to cry but the numbness that has taken over makes her tears seem false to her, as if she has turned them on for the young Mountie's benefit.

He drifts off toward Robbie, who is searching his glove compartment on the off chance there might be an old pack of cigarettes. After answering his questions, Robbie thinks to ask about her car. "She can likely pick it up tomorrow afternoon," the Mountie tells him. "We'll haul it into P.A. in the morning, but they'll be done with it pretty quick." When he sees she has quit weeping, he says to her, "It will be at the compound." He waves at Robbie as if he were some distance away. "You both have to come in anyway to make statements. Somebody'll give you a call tomorrow." As he pockets his notebook, his police radio makes a crackling noise and he goes to answer it. "Aw, jeez." He makes no effort to lower his voice. "I'm out here on my own. Yeah, I know. Frickin' reserve's only a few minutes away. I guess I'm it. Get Cecil to meet me out there." He nods at Lisa. "I've got to go. You two can go home now," he says, as if he's been holding them for interrogation. She feels oddly grateful he used the word 'frickin'. It shows he is conscious of his role in the community.

When he has driven off as far as the grid road, the siren begins an eerie wail, its final fading away leaving the countryside so still her ears ring. "A busy man," she says. Robbie doesn't answer. They stand on the edge of the field watching a wheat crop ripple like lake water in the starlight. "You'd better call Marjorie," she says.

"Marjorie and the twins are in Calgary visiting her sister again."

"Oh." A slight awkwardness shuffles onto the scene.

Robbie waves off a couple of early mosquitoes. "Let's get the hell out of here," he says. "Find somewhere else to have that drink."

He drives a short distance down the road, stopping at an old picnic site. She can see the outline of a table and benches, but inertia has taken hold and neither of them makes a move to get out. Robbie hands her the thermos bottle.

After a couple of good swallows, the violin strings of her nerves begin to relax. The rye is warm and bitter, but she wants to guzzle the lot of it. She sinks back into the truck's spongy bench seat. "Christ, what a night," she says.

"No kidding." Robbie takes a giant swig. Hogging it, she thinks.

She tells herself not to, but after a few drinks she begins once more to cry. Robbie reaches over awkwardly to pat her shoulder. "There, there," he says.

"Really?" She finds a Kleenex. After all that, after this whole night, suicide, the Holocaust, the mystery of human life and its misery. "Did you just say 'there, there'?"

Robbie gives a strangled guffaw, sounding as if someone has punched him in the stomach. "There, there," she repeats, and hilarity strikes her too until she holds her sides, weeping now with laughter. "How much?" she struggles to ask. "How much rye did you leave in the bottle anyway?"

Robbie is wiping his eyes now, trying to breathe. "Why? You want to go back for more?"

"It's just that I hope you left some so it doesn't look suspicious."

He clears his throat, sobered for a second. "None," he says. "I didn't leave any."

"None? You fool!" This sets them off again, until Robbie, subsiding once more, says, "Lisa."

She sniffs. He pulls her toward him and kisses her. Not thinking at all, of anything, she responds, her hand automatically travelling down from his chest until she encounters the sobering breadth of his stomach. She sits up. "This is not good," she says, definite. She shifts back toward the window on her side.

"Yeah." He breathes something between a sigh and a groan and coughs. "Aw, shit. Sorry."

"We've had too much to drink," she says. She wants to console him. He's been so helpful. "And after all we've been through."

They continue to share the rye. In spite of the amorous moment, Robbie relaxes easily back into neighbourly friendliness. She takes comfort from it. She promises herself she'll start inviting him and Marjorie over again. She's reminded of Marjorie's story about his emus, and decides what the hell. "Marjorie told me once…" She hesitates.

"Told you what?" He sounds so deeply suspicious that she hastens to reassure him.

"Just about what happened with your emus."

"Oh. Well."

"She wouldn't tell me how you killed them when shooting didn't work."

"It's no big secret," he says. But he doesn't continue.

"So?"

He heaves a jaded-sounding sigh, as if she's asked him about his income tax. "Like Marjorie probably told you, shooting some of them in the head didn't do a thing. Even in a sectioned-off part of the corral, they just wouldn't die. And the ones we had to butcher for meat…" He stops, looks down at his hands. "We finally used baseball bats. Worked like a charm." He clears his throat. "No, but it did the job. After a while of it we got punch drunk, yelling, "Steeerike one! And so on." He takes another swig. "I was gutted for a long time after."

"God." She tries to think of something to say.

"I'd thought of them as my ticket out. Out of debt and all that. They were, yeah, my big plan. What a way to end it." He lets Lisa drain the last couple of drops. "Have you ever been in a slaughterhouse?" he asks.

"No."

He cranes his neck to look out the windshield at the sky. A small cloud covering the moon is outlined in silver radiance. "We don't treat animals too good in general," he says. "Maybe it's something to do with the law of the jungle."

She recalls reading about an American professor who was able to design slaughterhouses that were more humane, less traumatic for the livestock because she was autistic and could identify with the way cattle perceive things. She is too tired to ask Robbie if he's heard of her. What was her name? Temple somebody. She smooths her mussed hair with her fingers. The body is a temple. Temple: the name of a Faulkner character, wasn't it? The one raped by some psychopath with a dried corn cob. Christ. The human race is nothing if not monstrous. "The Nazis slaughtered *people*." She says this abruptly, dismaying herself. "People like Ben Meisner, and treated them way worse than animals." Before he can ask anything, she says, "He told me his memories of that time and I can't bear to repeat them. But I asked him about it. I wanted to know. And now I guess dredging it all up killed him." She says this now as deadpan truth, dry-eyed.

"Don't take this on yourself, Lisa," Robbie says. "He was old and not well. He was ready to go, like you said when we found him."

"I know." Yes. She recalls saying something like that when her initial reaction to the suicide was anger. But anger has evaporated along with the shock, leaving nothing but sadness, a sense of being both brittle and limp, like a leaf in November and here it is, only spring. She needs another drink, but the thermos is empty.

"We'd better get going," Robbie says. "I'll pick you up tomorrow, whenever they tell us to come in." He starts the truck. "You'll be okay on your own?" He doesn't look at her.

"Oh yes," she says. She fastens her seatbelt.

SEVENTEEN

"He probably died sometime in the afternoon," Robbie says over the phone; the car had been running most of the day.

"Oh," she says.

"The cops said you didn't answer their call this morning. We're supposed to be in P.A. by two."

She takes four aspirin with her coffee and forces herself to ingest Pepto Bismol and dry toast for lunch. She sends Gerhardt an email, giving him an outline of recent events. She takes a couple of Tylenol for good measure. By the time Robbie shows up, she is able to function, but only just.

"I feel like hell," she says, climbing into his truck. Robbie, on the other hand, seems the same as usual. The picture of health, she thinks, conjuring a frame around his high-coloured face.

"Rye," he says. "Too bad Ben wasn't a gin drinker. It wouldn't have been as toxic."

"How selfish of him." She gives him a look. This day is going to be horrible. She'll be lucky if she doesn't throw up once they get to the police station. "Of course," she admits, "the wine I added to the mix when I got home didn't do me any good."

Robbie grins. "Tsk, tsk," he says, pronouncing it as if he were a kid reading from a cartoon speech balloon. He presses a button to open her window from his side, letting rejuvenating spring air blow onto her face. One thing about men, she thinks, grateful for the ensuing silence, they almost always make good drinking buddies. She closes her window. She doesn't want her hair to look like a bird's nest by the time they get there.

At the police station they sit in a busy waiting area between open offices and desks set up, it seems, randomly. A young Indigenous woman and an old man sit waiting with them. He asks Robbie a mumbled question ending with the word cigarette, and Robbie says, joshing him, "Yeah, I don't mind if I do. I've been craving a smoke for two days now."

The old man shakes his head. "No," he says clearly, "I said have you *got* a cigarette? Jodi here won't let me have any." He nods toward the young woman.

"No such luck," Robbie says.

"You can't smoke in here anyways." Jodi points to a large No Smoking sign.

"I know that." The old man gives her a disgusted look. "I'd take it outside."

She unearths a pack of Player's from an oversized leather handbag. "Here." She gives a cigarette to the old man and one to Robbie. "Knock yourselves out." She refuses Robbie's offered loonie and goes back to perusing an old *Reader's Digest*.

The thought of smoking turns Lisa's stomach. She looks around for something to read and asks Jodi, who points to a stack of *Reader's Digests* hidden behind a giant coffee urn. Paging through one that's five years old, she starts with "Laughter, the Best Medicine." *Two psychiatrists meet on the street. One says to the other, "You're fine. How am I?"*

Before she can turn to "Humor in Uniform," the main office door opens and a bald Mountie with official-looking insignia on his jacket comes out leading a grey-haired, heavy-set woman holding a Kleenex to her nose and crying. The Mountie gives a brief nod to Lisa. "Mrs. Braun? I'll be with you in a minute."

The woman stops cold, glaring at Lisa across the small passageway. "So you're the idiot," she says, her tear-smothered voice barely intelligible. "Why on earth would you lend him a car? We took away his licence years ago!" Mute with shame and defensive anger, Lisa can't reply. His daughter's voice rises and clarifies. "Didn't you even ask anyone? How could anybody be so stupid!?"

Lisa wants to say, So where were you all this time? but she continues to gaze at her magazine, conscious mainly of the dusty rose of the woman's pantsuit as she stands there for an eternity before rushing out the door.

She aches as if from a physical attack. What the hell was Ben Meisner's daughter doing here? Wouldn't the relatives just be sent to the morgue or somewhere to identify the body and make funeral arrangements? God, and she'd sat there looking down like a moron, like some kid getting heck. She could at least have said something.

She could have said she was sorry. Her throat swells into a dam she is afraid won't hold. Looking up, she sees that the Mountie is afraid of this too. He hands her a Styrofoam cup of black coffee and sits her down in his office. "Drink this," he directs. "I'll be back in a couple of minutes." His face is set into such a rictus of apprehension that a tiny back section of her mind lights up. He really, really hates this kind of thing, she thinks. Dealing with weeping women. And where is Robbie? Still outside, shooting the breeze with Gramps.

She has a choice. She can let herself feel so bad that she'll take an hour to quit crying, or she can get a grip. She forces the lukewarm brew down her throat, along with more Pepto Bismol. By the time the Mountie returns, she is, more or less calmly, reading "Life's Like That."

She gives him the same information she told the young constable last night, and knows before her story is finished she is in the clear. Not that she expected trouble, but the police could have made it more difficult, might even have considered the possibility of assisted suicide. Or at the very least, given her a fine for lending her car to someone with no licence. As it is, she can see he is merely going through the motions. He's already done with her, maybe because he's grateful to her for not making a scene.

He stands up to see her out the door. "I'll be a few minutes with Mr. Danielson here and then he can take you to pick up your car." Robbie is now sitting, restless and fidgeting, holding a magazine he isn't looking at. He disappears with the Mountie into his office.

It's upsetting to be reminded of her car, reminded she has to drive it home now after a body lay in the back seat all of yesterday. But she holds herself in, keen to get out of here. Waiting for Robbie, she gives up on the *Reader's Digest* after going through an entire article about skydiving without comprehending a thing.

She doesn't know she is staring off into space right at the girl sitting across from her until Jodi asks, "Are you doing okay there?"

"Oh! Sorry, I'm just..." She looks down.

"So what was all that about, anyway, that lady yelling at you?"

She clears her throat. "I let her old dad borrow my car and he, uh...he died in it. So I had to come and pick it up today." Here she is, being sociable again. She should have said she didn't want to talk about it.

"That your husband?" The girl nods at the office door Robbie went through.

"No. My neighbour."

"From P.A.?"

"Cullen." She decides what the hell. The girl is just being friendly, and talking is, after all, a distraction. "And you? Are you from here?"

"Yeah." Jodi glances at the old man now dozing beside her, then nods toward another door. "My granddad and me, we're waiting for my auntie and a couple of her friends. They flew in from Caribou Point a few days ago and went on a bender."

"Caribou Point? My husband's up there! He's teaching a new computer system he installed in the high school."

Jodi looks at her with new interest. "Gerhardt somebody?"

"Yes. Braun."

"My aunt's in his computer class."

"No kidding? Small world, eh?" Jesus, what is she thinking, choosing this moment to become Chatty Cathy.

"She likes him." Jodi puts her magazine down beside her, ready for more information. "He's a real character, she says."

"Really. I don't know about that." She knows how virulent gossip is in the North. Now the story about Gerhardt's wife, the suspicious death of someone in her car, will spread like a flu virus, mutating into scandal along the way. And what the hell does Gerhardt think he's doing, becoming a character?

Robbie's on his way out now, saying something rueful to the sergeant. Corporal. Whatever he is. What with all the commotion, she can't recall him introducing himself. As she gets ready to leave, she notices she's been clutching her purse strap so hard its outline is legible in the palm of her hand.

The old man shifts in his chair, awake again. "Take it easy, eh," he advises Robbie. Robbie nods and says he always does. Lisa says a quick goodbye to Jodi and follows him out the door.

At the compound, after she signs a form, a scrawny man who looks as if he's just rolled out of bed leads them to her car. "She's all set to go," he says, scratching his head as he hands her the keys. She thanks him, but then just stands there. The man sidles up to her confidentially. "No clean up necessary."

"Well. Yes, that's good." Does he mean they'd cleaned it up for her, or that it wasn't necessary in the first place? He remains standing expectantly beside her, so she unlocks the door and gets in. She waves at Robbie.

"I'll follow you home," he says.

She turns the ignition and opens the window. "No. You've done enough. I'll be fine, just go and do your errands and I'll drive home on my own."

Relief flashes across his face, immediately stifled by concern. "Are you sure?" He says this a bit too loudly, as if the window were still closed. She nods. "I'll call you later in the day then, after I get in from spraying," he says.

"Good." She gives a slight wave to both men as she navigates carefully out of her parking space. Poor Robbie, now having to go home and spread fertilizer or herbicide. She's kept him from almost a whole day's farming, which he can ill afford at this time.

She lied when she said she was fine. She can smell something—could it be death?—and keeps the window open. But at a gas station a few blocks away, she manages to fill up using self-serve. She wonders if the police filled the car with a jerry can and drove it to Prince Albert, or had it towed. There was enough gas in the tank to drive away from the compound. Thinking about gas, carrying out the chore of procuring it, has a calming effect, although once she finds herself on the highway she notices the telephone poles whizz by so quickly that she makes herself slow down. She doesn't want anything more to do with the police.

She dreads having to call Gerhardt but knows she should tell him today that one of his students would know all about this disaster. Or at least know that someone had died in her car. She represses an urge to glance at the back seat. Then again, Gerhardt isn't one to care much about gossip, as long as people mind their own business to his face.

But he will be disturbed, deeply upset with her. She has brought this between them, unearthed his country's disgrace from its carefully buried oblivion and, not leaving it at that, became obsessed, digging for more and more, unable to rest until confronted with the tragedy it deserved.

••

"SO DO YOU want me to come home?" Gerhardt isn't angry, or sympathetic for that matter, but hesitant, reluctant to immerse himself in her unhappiness, or in any of it. As she expected, he considers this a mess of her own making, and in fact knows that any comfort he could articulate would seem inadequate to her, casting him into, as he would put it, a lose–lose situation.

"No. Just finish your contract. It's only a couple more weeks. If your student asks about what happened, all I told her niece was that he died in my car. You can say he had a heart attack or something."

"Ach, I could give a shit about all that. Gossip is so much more interesting than the truth, no one will bother me to find out any facts."

The truce. One thing for sure, Gerhardt would not want to hear about Ben Meisner's experiences. Eventually, after enough silence, their marriage would likely go on as usual. They'd travel somewhere warm next winter, and she would vow, never again.

EIGHTEEN

A funeral ceremony is held for Ben Meisner at a synagogue in Prince Albert. Lisa does not attend. She mourns the loss of a new friend, mourns the tragedy of his history and its consequences, feels she has as much right to be there as any of his neighbours. But she doesn't want to risk seeing his daughter again.

Marjorie comes over for coffee, and after the initial shocked sympathy, chats about local gossip and the continuing ups and downs of their plans for the family reunion. Alice Jointon phones, wondering if Lisa could give someone a ride next Tuesday, and adding that they could use someone to weed the flower beds. "No one blames you for Ben's…uh…We all just wish you the best and hope now that you started volunteering, you can continue on with us."

"That's nice of you to say, Alice, but I'm done. Sorry."

She is always disturbed by night sweats, and she still often stays awake worrying. About Stephanie, of course, the old regrets and sad anxieties circling for hours, familiar bats in the belfry of her mind, but also now about Tyler and Céline. She is aware more than ever that all kinds of things can happen, especially in big cities in Europe. She finally falls asleep toward morning, sometimes dreaming about Ben Meisner.

Sitting on her front deck in the afternoon, she notices a laziness that is familiar, more like her old self. Dirty dishes have multiplied on the kitchen counter; dust clouds the sections of coffee table not covered by books and old magazines; slut's wool eddies under the furniture. She thinks about phoning one of the school board offices for work, but it's too late in June. She'll wait and see what September brings in the way of mental health.

Appreciating the warmth of the sunlight, she begins to admire the colours in her garden, notes with renewed interest that the orange lilies she planted last fall clash with the maroon buds of her old peony. She'll move the lilies in October. She should find her garden notebook.

As she sits amid lengthening afternoon shadows, she feels a lack. She should be holding the stem of a wine glass. She could drive into Cullen, to the hotel bar there. Wine is likely part of their off-sale—she doesn't have to drive all the way to the liquor store in P.A. She needs groceries again too. She'll drive into town, stop at the gas station and The Store Formerly Known as Co-op, as Robbie calls it, and pick up wine and maybe some beer at the hotel.

Halfway down the driveway she realizes she's neglected to close the garage door, but she keeps going, down the gravel road past the Danielsons' white two-storey, on past other farms to the highway, past acreages with newer houses of earth-toned stucco whose owners she doesn't know. She slows to the speed limit. Maturing crops frame oval sloughs reflecting blue sky and clouds; poplar leaves flash silvery undersides in the wind. She relaxes into the scenery. The town of Cullen appears far too soon, but she follows the curve of the turnoff, tires crackling on the gravel, past aging bicoloured bungalows, past the vast empty lot where the grain elevator used to stand. She stops at the gas station and waits. Eventually, a kid she's thankful not to know saunters out the front door. As she tells him to fill it up, she realizes she doesn't want to get out of the car to use her credit card, so counts her cash.

Once that chore is done, she drives the few feet to the faded false front of the store. An enervating mist settles on her as she sits there anticipating the store owner's friendly questions about how her husband is doing up north, chit-chat about how well the crops are coming along. Comments, maybe, on what a shame about Ben Meisner. She drives to the hotel instead, to what the locals still call the beer parlour. Parked in front of the bar entrance, she continues to sit in the car until a heavy young man in a baseball hat and plaid flannel shirt walks past and waves at her. One of her random students from a few years ago, he farms now just outside of town. She opens her window. "Hello!" What the hell is his name?

"Hi, Mrs. Braun. How're you doing?" He grins and waves again, ready to enter the bar.

"Could you do me a favour?" she calls. "I've kind of twisted my ankle and find it hard to get around. I wonder if you could buy me some white wine?" He ambles up to her car, nodding agreeably. Such a nice kid. Emptying her wallet, she finds sixty dollars and hands it to him. "Can you get however many bottles that will buy?"

"Sure," he says. "There's not much choice, but do you want the better stuff?"

"I guess so." Although maybe she should just load up on plonk. But she nods. "Yes. Go ahead, get something half-decent." She intended to use her Mastercard here and stock up, but that doesn't seem to be in the cards today, credit or not.

He comes back with three bottles nicely chilled from the bar fridge and change too paltry for her to tell him to keep. "Thank you so much!" Damn, what is his name? "Have a nice day." She gives a little wave as she drives off. Have a nice day? What is wrong with her?

Before heading out of town she picks up her mail since there's nobody at the post office, then continues on to Pioneer Lodge and pulls over to the side of the road. The three-storey box of a nursing home is becoming shabby, looking as provisional as an East German apartment building from the sixties. The rows of solid one-storey duplexes take up most of the property. When she sees that weeds are taking over Ben Meisner's lady's mantle and lilies, she thinks she will get out of the car and deal with them. But then his neighbour comes out and begins to tend her own front garden. Blindsided by a stab of grief, she turns the car around and heads for the highway.

As she drives off blacktop onto the grid road, the anticipation of reaching her house and opening a bottle of wine becomes so acute she has to make herself slow down. Finally driving down her driveway, she's faced with the ominous presence of a square black hole: the open door of her garage. She parks outside and manages to edge her way close enough to heave the door shut. Safe in the house again, she searches vainly for overhead door batteries. Another item to add to her grocery list. She unscrews the lid off a wine bottle and sips her first glass at the kitchen table.

Lorne. That's the name of the kid who bought the wine. Lorne Summerfield. What a nice name for a farmer. She holds the wine glass to the light, toasts him, and tries to remember something about him as a student but can only come up with the fact that she knows who he is. At any rate, she is grateful.

··

TYLER CALLS. He has news too important for an email, he says. "Oh god." Lisa feels the cold hand of more worry. "Céline's not pregnant!?"

"Yes! Yes, how did you know?"

"Tyler!" Excitement and a hard lump of anxiety lodge in the pit of her stomach. "Well as far as I know, she isn't susceptible to nausea, so when you talked about her not feeling well, I naturally thought of morning sickness. When is she due?"

"Around mid-January."

"Are you coming home?"

"We're thinking we'll move to Saskatoon in the fall."

"I'm so stunned I can't feel a thing," she says, but even as she speaks she feels the first stirrings of joy. "Have you told Dad yet?"

"No, I'd just get the school answering machine. Can you leave him a message to phone you? And then I'll email tomorrow."

"Are you happy? I mean you and Céline? I thought you two didn't want to bring any more children into this overpopulated world."

"Mom. We're really happy. It was planned, you know, more or less. Céline figured she was getting up there, biological clock and all that. You should see her."

She would see her all right. Along with her grandchild, she would have to acknowledge Céline Jenkins's presence in her world now forever. "Can I talk to her?"

"She's out with Tatyana right now. We'll call again in a few days maybe."

As she listens to their plans, the prospect of a baby begins to percolate everything out of her system but joy. It feels as if her own stomach has a touch of morning sickness. Before they hang up, Tyler says, "Remember what you asked me about in your email? About the Bulgarian character?"

"Oh." She doesn't want to be reminded of all that at this very moment. "Yes?"

"I discussed it with Marko and Tatyana. You know what they said?"

"What?" She tries to keep the irritation out of her voice.

"Well for one thing, it has to do with history. You know, like back in the old days the Jews here were innkeepers and that sort of thing, not moneylenders, and they've been in this region as long as the Bulgarians. It's not that they weren't separate, but they were always equal. And then, the people running the church here, the Eastern Orthodox? They weren't like the Catholic pope. They were brave, at least as church leaders go, and refused to co-operate with the Nazis. Plus, there was this one government guy who put his neck on the line to save the Jews. Peshev? Tatyana said her grandfather told her thousands of Jews were all set, all rounded up like in other countries to get onto the cattle cars for the death camps, and then because of this government guy, they were sent home."

"Peshev. Yes. But I read that the population, the ordinary people, wouldn't co-operate with the Nazis either."

"That's right. Tatyana's grandfather told her no one co-operated with them."

"But then how were the Jews rounded up? If no one co-operated?"

"Mom. I don't know. I suppose there were enough Nazi troops here to hunt them down. Or they were ordered to show up in the town square or wherever like in other places and they did. All I know is the ordinary Bulgarians refused to turn them in." He hesitates. "You know what Tatyana's grandfather said?"

"No," Lisa says. "I don't."

"Well, he's old you know. Doesn't care much about what he says, or maybe he's a bit senile. Anyway, he said, 'We didn't like Jews all that much either, but these were *our* Jews.' Céline thinks the Bulgarians didn't co-operate because they're just contrary. If you order them to do anything, you might as well forget about it."

"Are you going to stay in Bulgaria much longer? Will you be visiting Oma and Opa? You could stay in Berlin with Hanne and Peter."

"That's the plan, once Céline's morning sickness goes away altogether. We want to see France and Holland too. And England. We like it here because of our friends, but Sofia isn't that exciting. And I'm getting tired of all the boozing. That shitty *rakia*, the guys here guzzle it like water, even Marko."

"Céline, of course, isn't drinking anything, eh?"

"Mom. She's not a teenager you know."

••

"AT LEAST," she says on the phone to Gerhardt later, "Céline is a serious, sober type of person. She'll likely be a very good mom. I just hope she's getting enough protein. And now Tyler has to find a real job."

"They'll be okay, especially if they move to Saskatoon. It's Stephanie I'm worried about, but what else is new?" They discuss the kids, reminisce, make predictions and plans for their grandchild. Their acreage is a perfect place for him to spend part of the summer. They could drive to the lake, take him canoeing. Or her. She could run around in the yard or explore the bush. Maybe they'll get another dog.

Suzanne emails to say she'll be coming in August to put her condo up for sale and wrap up the details of her move. She hopes she can stay with Lisa and Gerhardt for a few days. Lisa should come and visit, spend a week or two this year in Guelph. Or maybe they could share a vacation somewhere.

Stephanie phones. "Hi, Mom."

"Stephanie!"

"How are *you*?" Stephanie asks.

"Fine," she says. She wishes Stephanie didn't sound so much like a telemarketer whenever she wants something. "So, how are *you* doing?"

"Uh, okay." Stephanie hesitates, her tone changing. "Like, not that great I guess."

The old despair freezes her initial pleasure at hearing her daughter's voice. How much does she want? "What's the problem?"

Stephanie hesitates, and Lisa can almost hear gears turning. "Oh, I wanted to ask how you were doing, Mom. Like are you still looking up those websites?"

"No, I'm fine now. I feel well and I'm gardening and all that."

"I'm thinking I might come home for a while," Stephanie says bluntly.

Home. "Like Saskatoon, you mean?"

"I mean with you and Dad."

"Oh."

"Kelvin sort of...uh, him and I haven't worked out, like we split up. I was thinking of leaving here anyway."

Of course. "And I suppose you never did register for any classes?"

"Yeah well, like, that didn't work out either."

Disappointment paralyzes the back of Lisa's throat. She lets her silence speak until Stephanie says, "Mom?"

She croaks a noncommittal yes.

"Is Dad around?"

"He's still working up north. We're not sending you any money. Don't even ask. This has been going on too long, Stephanie, you'll be thirty years old before you know it. The most I can do is get you a bus ticket. Then once you're here you can look for a job and find a place in P.A. or Saskatoon."

It's Stephanie's turn to be silent.

What is she doing? Now she's committed herself to taking her daughter in, one more time. "That's it. Take it or leave it." Stephanie would email Gerhardt and try to convince him to transfer money over the net.

"Okay," Stephanie says tonelessly.

"You can pick up the ticket at the bus depot there in a couple of days."

"Okay, bye then, Mom. Love ya."

"Me too. Goodbye, Stephanie." Stephanie had begun to sign off with "love ya" even before her suave drug personality manifested itself because kids and parents said it on TV all the time. Lisa's own parents knew she loved them without her having to say it, and its casual use always makes her uncomfortable. Now it sounds sarcastic.

With a twinge of pain at the top of her stomach (does that mean an ulcer?), she realizes she didn't even talk about Tyler and Céline, didn't think of mentioning to Stephanie that she would soon be an aunt.

For the remainder of the day she's left with the familiar despair, a daytime version of her night insomnia, recycling with hindsight the old disappointments and disasters regarding Stephanie she so hoped were behind her, uneasily hopeful that a new location and some education would transform into useful life experience. Hope, that last evil in the box.

So now she has to take care of the bus ticket. Getting ready to drive into P.A., she notices with disgust her unmade bed, the overflowing laundry basket blocking the way to the mirror beside the dresser. She'll throw in a load before she leaves. As she carries the basket downstairs, all the times that Stephanie broke her heart, dashed her hopes, all those clichés of maternal disappointment seethe under her skin, feeding a sudden energy. She will do all the chores she's been putting off. She stuffs white towels and sheets in the washing machine and turns it on. Hardly thinking about it, she opens the newly dusted basement closet, finds the leather SS coat, and wraps it around an old brick she uses as a doorstop.

She drives to P.A. so calmly, with such efficiency, she doesn't bother to use cruise control. Crops are coming along well this year. Soft brushes of maturing barley glow in the sunlight, transforming the landscape on both sides of the highway into a silver-green sea. Gerhardt will be home soon.

In Prince Albert, she takes care of Stephanie's ticket at the bus depot, buys groceries, stocks up at the liquor store, tops up the gas in the car, and drives with crisp confidence through the car wash. Using the coin-operated vacuum, she cleans the inside of the car. There's no sign that anything happened in the back seat, but she buys some upholstery shampoo to use later. Along the river park across the street from Suzanne's condo, she hikes to a small lookout point over the water, the wind gusting so strongly she wishes she'd brought a headscarf.

Although it rained only a day ago, the air seems dusty. Because of the leaves, she realizes. The city elms and poplars, the ashes, are all showing their leaves' undersides in the wind, seeming to scatter the atmosphere with greyish green. Compared to the washed-out blue of the sky, the choppy water looks vibrant, radiating its own deep, almost navy blue. A sign leaning against the riverbank warns of thin ice. At this time of day, joggers and walkers are at work, and nobody is around to see her throw the overcoat into the Saskatchewan River. She brushes away an image of Ben Meisner's parents falling through darkness and makes her way to a bench. She cranes her neck to stare across the road at Suzanne's empty balcony and thinks maybe she should try to convince Gerhardt to move back to Saskatoon, especially now that Tyler and Céline plan to live there with their grandchild.

At home again, she decides the mess in her house has to be cleaned. She pushes the vacuum joylessly around the living room, arranges dishes in the dishwasher, and makes a few swipes at her furniture with a duster. Clean all the corners and the centre will take care of itself. She should call Aunt Gemma while she still can. Tell her about Tyler's baby. Once in a while she has a good day, the people in the nursing home say, and maybe she's having one now.

"Yes!" A relentlessly cheerful voice tells her Gemma is sitting outside in the sun in her wheelchair. "Hold on, I'll give her the phone. She's a real livewire right now. She'll be happy to hear from you."

"Hello?"

"Aunt Gemma! It's Lisa. How are you?"

"Oh," Gemma says vaguely. "Lisa?"

"Yes, it's me! I was cleaning the house and thought of how you always kept everything so nice."

"I did?" Gemma's voice is soft and cracked with age.

"Yes. Your house was always spotless. And your garden perfect too. I'm so interested in gardening now, you know. I wish you could see mine. Well, I think I showed you pictures last time I was in Regina." She goes on a bit too long describing flowers, not wanting to hear that Gemma has no idea who's on the line.

The old woman's voice sinks to a whisper. "Lisa?" Silence. Then she speaks up. "I just slapped a mosquito. I'm sitting beside a pot of flowers, and if I concentrate just on these very petunias, I can pretend I'm in your garden."

"Ha, like that poem, Aunt Gemma! 'To make a prairie it takes a clover and one bee.'"

"You always read so much, Lisa. We were happy to see you take teacher training."

"I'm still teaching, subbing mainly in Prince Albert."

"Oh yes. Prince Albert?" Silence. "Who is this?"

"It's Lisa."

"Oh yes?" The phone makes a couple of clicking sounds.

"Uh-oh," the cheerful aide comes on the line. "She's dropped off for a nap."

"That's fine," Lisa says. She would tell her about the baby next time. "We had a lovely chat. Thank you so much."

"Any time! Actually morning is usually the best, but she did well today. Bye now."

"Goodbye."

She sits down at the kitchen table and wipes her eyes. To make a garden it takes a flower and one mosquito.

A few days later, Stephanie calls. She has the bus ticket but has decided to put off coming home. She has found another serving job and can stay for a couple of months with a friend. So, like, she cashed in the ticket and would likely hitch a ride home sometime in the fall before the weather turns cold. Lisa tells Stephanie about the baby, and Stephanie says she knows, that Tyler texted her, isn't that great.

..

LISA SPENDS the next day in the garden spreading a layer of leaf mould she dug from under the poplar trees. The composted mulch crumbles like chocolate sponge cake in her hands, as dark and earthy as the primal satisfaction of gardening itself. They will not move back to Saskatoon. A grandchild could spend weeks on end here, as she used to with her aunt and uncle in La Ronge. She could teach her to garden. She would read to her from all the beloved kids' books stored in the basement. In the midst of filling another wheelbarrow, she sees a white sedan pull up in front of the house. Peering through the branches of what she now calls the emu tree, she supposes it is Marjorie. They must have bought a new vehicle. She claps the excess soil from her hands and prepares to convince her neighbour that she is fine. She had cabin fever, was depressed by her research, and unhinged by Ben Meisner and his death, but she is over all that. She is cured. Ignoring a brief image of cured ham studded with cloves, she emerges from the bush at the same time as the driver gets out of her car. It isn't Marjorie, but a heavy, grey-haired woman a few years past her own age. "Oh fuck." She says it aloud, but the visitor is already on the doorstep, likely too far away to hear. After instinctively turning back toward the tree, she forces herself to walk out to the yard. "Hello?" she calls.

"Oh! Hello." The woman turns awkwardly, climbs down the steps as if they are precarious, and holds out her hand. "I'm Simone Lasky, Ben Meisner's daughter." Unlike her father, she pronounces Simone with two syllables.

"Yes." Lisa nods grimly. We met, she thinks but doesn't say. She displays her dirty hands as if giving herself up and adds, "Excuse me."

"I came to apologize." Simone takes a few steps forward to become a stolid presence directly in front of Lisa. "None of it was your fault. I know what my father did was his own choice." Her voice holds something of a practised quality, as if she has been rehearsing.

Lisa says she is sorry too, for her part in it. "And very sorry for your loss." She knows she sounds too cool, but she wants the woman gone. After an awkward pause, she goes on, "I'd invite you in but I'm in the middle of something I really need to get done."

"Oh no, that's fine." But Simone stands there, making no move toward her car. She wants to talk. Something of the old neurotic wretchedness begins to press the back of Lisa's neck. The woman gestures toward the deck chairs. "I wonder if we could sit outside here for a few minutes?"

"Of course." She leads the way to the deck. What else can she do?

Once seated, Simone gazes at the garden but doesn't mention it. "I understand that my father recounted…" She stops. "I heard from the police that he told you about his experiences in Buchenwald."

"Yes. Yes he did."

"He would only ever tell us about his escape over the border and some of what happened in Denmark and Sweden."

"I know."

"I saw his scars. Or caught glimpses of them when I was a child. He wouldn't talk about how he got them or any of it. I would like to know what he went through. I'm aware of the horrors from other people's accounts, but I would like to know. About him. What he told you."

"Oh." Lisa stares off at the garden, more or less at the same spot Simone seems to be examining, a barren patch near the compost bin. She senses that if she sits here in silence, Simone will wait with monolithic patience past sunset and on into the next morning. "I'll write something," she says. This would give her a reprieve. "Give me your address or email and I'll send you an account of the facts, which is all I have. I can't duplicate the way he told me about it. He described what happened, not so much how he felt under, uh…He said focusing on details would force him to relive them, would cause them to expand, like a sponge soaking up water, until they filled his whole being."

Simone turns toward her as a blind person might, hearing a voice she knows. "He would put it like that. Make some metaphor."

Parents are able to annoy well beyond the grave, Lisa thinks. "He told it all with a certain calmness, but it was very disturbing. Not that he was dispassionate. As I said, I won't be able to reproduce anything like him actually sitting there, saying those things."

"No. Of course not." Simone seems to have no intention of leaving.

If they are going to sit here any longer, she'll need a drink. "I'm going in to wash my hands, and I'd like a glass of wine. Would you like one?"

Simone gives an unsurprised nod. "Sure."

"I'm afraid I'm no connoisseur," Lisa says, although she knows the bottle chilling in the fridge is Sauvignon Blanc. "I have either dry white or red."

"Any white will do, thanks."

After returning with the wine, she asks, "What kind of work do you do?" She might as well make conversation. Simone would linger now at least as long as it took to finish her glass.

"I'm a nurse, like my mother was." Her expression clears briefly. "I'm thinking of taking early retirement, although there's such a shortage I could stay on part time until I drop."

The afternoon continues to wane in small talk and silences. Lisa still resents Simone for what she put her through at the police station, and Simone can't hide the fact that she is still angry, and jealous as well. It is Lisa who has been told. Lisa who knows the traumas, the horrors that were the roots of Ben Meisner's life. She wonders if Simone knows about her father's talk with his granddaughter in the hospital. She's tempted to ask outright, even to compare notes on difficult daughters. But there is something precarious about the woman. Something needy and off-balance that she knows enough not to encourage by knocking down barriers. "I never thought to ask your dad if he and your mother took any trips. Did they ever go back to Denmark or Sweden?"

"No. They could have afforded to after they sold the farm, but they didn't go. They went to Arizona a couple of winters soon after they retired, but I don't think they ever wanted to set foot in Europe again."

"He must have been grateful to the Danes all his life though."

"Grateful. Yes he was, of course. But he had no great opinion of them as heroic. He said the Germans liked them, and they liked the Germans. Some of them joined the Nazi army, to fight the Soviets, they said later."

"But they refused to turn in their Jewish citizens."

"They did, yes, and that was of course remarkable. Heroic." Simone takes a sip of wine and sets the glass down carefully on the wooden arm of the Adirondack chair. "But then there was no reign of terror there. Oh, if you ask the Danes, they'll come up with bitter memories like everyone else. But they weren't put to the test as profoundly as so many other countries. They were ideal Aryan types, and the Nazis admired them."

"Didn't they... They all got together, the whole country networking to make it possible to ferry the Jews over to Sweden. Before any of them could be rounded up by the Germans. Israel honoured the entire country as Righteous Among the Nations."

"Of course, yes, the Danes showed bravery then, and great goodwill. Some of them also charged an arm and a leg for the use of their boats. But yes, that's beside the point, they still did it."

She wonders if Simone knows somehow that she is part Danish. She takes a sip of wine, waiting for her to say something more. Then she replies, "It's not that famous a story with the rest of the world, the Danes helping their Jewish citizens escape. My father was Danish, but I only learned about it from reading Hannah Arendt and then looking it up."

"Oh yes, Arendt," Simone is about to say something but then seems to think better of it. "Heidegger's girlfriend."

"Yes." Lisa doesn't want to sound clueless; she knows Heidegger kept his job under the Nazi regime, and that it was partly because of Arendt's support that he managed to rehabilitate his reputation afterwards. She knows Arendt's book offended many Jews, that only recently has the worth of her insights been better accepted. But now she wishes she had kept stubbornly silent. She has done very little research, in the scheme of things. Why get into any of this with Simone?

She tips her wine glass to taste the last few drops, and to emphasize that she is finished. This conversation can go nowhere. She wants Simone to go away, doesn't want to have to deal with her, and doesn't want to gaze any further into the vast cavern of her own ignorance. She will never know enough, can never know as much as someone with Simone's background who has likely been studying her own heritage all her life.

She recalls Primo Levi's quote. Existing words "are free words, created and used by free men who lived in comfort and suffering in their own homes." There can be no words, no understanding, no answers, and certainly no way of sanitizing the filth of the Holocaust. No matter how often she cleans, no matter how hard she scrubs and polishes.

Watching her, Simone takes a pen and a piece of paper out of her purse. "Here's my address, phone number, and email."

Lisa folds it into her jeans pocket. "Listen," she says, regretting her promise, resenting the woman's expectations, her stifled anger, and the sense that Simone is disappointed in her. "I'm not going to have a deadline for this. It may be a month or a year. Or..." She shrugs and leaves it at that.

"I see. Yes." After a long pause, Simone says, "Buchenwald affected all of us, his family. He told us nothing of the camp, but we grew up fearful because of it. And strangely, we were told crazy and personal things about his escape to Denmark. Did he tell you about the other time he tried to kill himself?"

"No!"

"Not here in Canada, but back then. It was when he was still hiding in that forest." She shakes her head. "He tried to hang himself from a tree near the hut with the belt from his coat, but it didn't hold. He told about it with a certain humour. He'd picked the one branch on the whole tree that had a rotten core. He found himself fallen into a pile of old leaves, looking up at the sky, and decided to live out his life." She clears her throat. "Until now. I never understood why he tried to kill himself back then. He must have fought so hard for life all through that concentration camp, and then when he had the chance to leave it behind and live, he chose death." She shrugs her shoulders, for a moment resembling her father. "That's just one of the many things I may never know about him."

"Did he ever say what happened to his parents?" Shocked at herself, Lisa decides she can't backtrack. "Your grandparents?"

"They died during the war, but that's really all we know. I think he felt so bad leaving them behind that he couldn't bear to talk about them."

"Didn't you ever try to find out?" Something is urging her on. The desire to tell.

"Yes, my brother Ben did. He learned that they both died quite early on, but that's all." She sees a shift in the woman's expression. Maybe she knows more than she is willing to say. But if so, why would she still wonder about that suicide attempt in the forest? Simone stands abruptly, motioning Lisa to remain in her chair. "I hope to hear from you before too long," she says.

"Wait," Lisa says. "I should have mentioned this before. I don't know if you're aware of it, but your father once talked to your daughter. He said he told her something of what went on in Buchenwald. This was when she was a teenager. I think you should ask her what she remembers."

Simone remains standing on the deck looking down at her, frozen for a long moment, her expression one of indecision rather than surprise. Finally she says, "I don't see my daughter anymore. But yes." Then she leaves, driving off without saying goodbye.

Lisa has no idea if she can bring herself to write anything down, or if so, what she will include. Simone knows something about her grandparents, but likely just that they killed themselves. What good would it do to write the truth, to bestow it now on Ben Meisner's family like an ugly heirloom? It wouldn't mean she'd be rid of it. No, she should keep her silence regarding his parents because she promised him she would, and he'd been her friend.

Too tired to go back to the garden, she trails inside, planning to take a nap, but then she recalls the nightmare from the last nap she'd taken. Jack Cennon trying to interview her. While she pours herself another glass of wine, the phone rings. Caribou Point. She lets it ring. The thought of chatting amiably with Gerhardt right now seems inconceivable. The house is silent; the kitchen clock scrapes her nerves with its tick, tick, reminding her of an old joke: *Vee haf vays of makink you tock.*

She sits down at the computer, wanting to find distraction if not solace. She glances over her search history, intending to look at some innocuous interest from the time before. Before she knew Ben Meisner existed. There. Max Ernst, *Lunar Asparagus.* She will search, even if fruitlessly, for something cheerful. A new site pops up, a virtual tour of New York's Museum of Modern Art. Good.

She scrolls past rows of squares the size of postage stamps, pictures of sculptures and paintings, until she is caught by the name Ernst. She finds images of his work, finally sees the outline she's looking for on the screen in miniature. Enlarging the photo, she finds her *Lunar Asparagus.* There it is, set on the floor of the museum, looking up at her exactly as she saw it the first time. True, the other one, the goggle-eyed triangle, stands alongside. But her asparagus stalk exists just as she remembers, its white eyeless face lit by a grin signifying such bliss in the cosmic infinity of its own idiocy she can only shake her head in wonder.

ACKNOWLEDGEMENTS

Before I had any idea I would write *The Beech Forest*, I researched the Holocaust to try to understand something, anything at all, about the incomprehensible. Over the years, I have read Primo Levi, Elie Wiesel, Gitta Sereny, Hannah Arendt, Daniel Goldhagen and others, and fiction by many writers. I have found various websites, some of which no longer exist. *The Buchenwald Report* (edited and translated by David A. Hackett, Westview Press, 1995) provided vital information for the story of my fictional survivor. The quote from the Mengele survivor, although also fiction, was inspired by testimonials published on the Claims Conference's website (www.claimscon.org), as part of their work to seek recompense for those who survived Nazi medical experimentation.

I would like to thank the Saskatchewan Arts Board for the grant supporting a revision of this novel; Connie Gault and Dianne Warren for their invaluable critical advice; and Thistledown Press for their faith in this book and for providing my patient and insightful editor, Michael Kenyon.

ACKNOWLEDGEMENT OF QUOTATIONS

Excerpt from *Survival in Auschwitz: The Nazi Assault on Humanity*, p. 123, by Primo Levi. Translated from the Italian by Stuart Woolf (New York: Simon & Schuster, 1996). *Survival in Auschwitz* originally appeared in English under the title *If This is a Man*.

Excerpt from *The Tunnel*, p. 155, by William H. Gass, Alfred A. Knopf, 1995 (Penguin Random House).

PHOTO: DON HALL

Born in Kinistino, Saskatchewan, Marlis Wesseler attended university in Saskatoon and Regina, taught school in the North, travelled extensively, and has lived and worked in Regina for over forty years. *The Beech Forest* is her sixth book of fiction. Award-winning and often nominated, her previous books are the short story collections *Life Skills* and *Imitating Art*, and the novels *Elvis Unplugged, South of the Border,* and *The Last Chance Ladies' Book Club.*